Taking Territory

Taking Territory

Keys to Posessing Your Promised Land

Dr. Jimmie A. Ellis

Cover Design By Maurice Jones of majonesdesigns.com

Printed in the United States of America

Publishing services by Selah Publishing Group, LLC, Tennessee. The views expressed or implied in this work do not necessarily reflect those of Selah Publishing Group.

ISBN: 978-1-58930-220-4
Library of Congress Control Number: 2008907261

Dedications

You can never take territory by yourself, so I would like to thank those who pushed me or played a special part in my taking territory past and present:

Bishop and Mother Myers, Lillian "Mom" Partlowe, Mt. Olive Church, Dan Brasher, Apostle Marva Strothers, Evangelist Yashima White, Elder Barbara Lester, Pastor Steven Walker, Bishop Don Meares, Dad, Grandmom (my cheerleaders), My grandfather - James Ellis Sr., John, Salina, nieces and nephews The "Boobies" - Joshua & Justin, My Protégés, Elders William and Virginia Booth, Dr. Wesley T. Proctor, Elder Theresa Settles, Deacons George and Betty Ligon

I dedicate this wonderful book to all my VCC family; you are the reason I want to take territory!!

Dr. Jimmie A. Ellis
TheBish08

Contents

Foreword ix

Introduction xi

Chapter One
This Territory is Mine 15

Chapter Two
Joshua's Five Secrets 29

Chapter Three
Too Selfish to Help Someone Else 45

Chapter Four
Territorial Trap One: *Territory Outside of God's Will* 59

Chapter Five
Territorial Trap Two: *Tedious Talking* 73

Chapter Six
Territorial Trap Three: *Tempting God* 79

Chapter Seven
Territorial Trap Four: *Tripping Into Sin* 83

Chapter Eight
Tools for Taking Territory:
How to Possess Your Promised Land 101

About the Author 117

Foreword

"It's not the will to win that matters—everyone has that. It's the will to prepare to win that matters." (Paul "Bear" Bryant)

I've known Dr. Ellis for more than twenty-five years. I can attest to the richness of the deposit of God's grace in his life. I've always known that he will not embarrass the grace of God in his life, but <u>Taking Territory: Keys to Possessing Your Promised Land</u> is beyond any message or written material Dr. Ellis has done before.

The above quotation signals what is on each page of this book. In this book is not mere information, reading for the sake of reading. It is filled with instructions about how to prepare to take territory. It is the how-to-manual for those really serious about obeying the word of the Lord wholly.

I cite Dr. Ellis from the book: "Territory is God working through you. You will have to learn that half the stuff that comes through your hand will not be for you. You are used to everything being for you all of the time. When you walk with God, He will let you know that you brought certain items to give them to someone else. You cannot act like it is yours because it is not. That is what taking territory is all about."

Dr. Ellis understands the Kingdom of God. He outlines the principle of territory in such a way that the mature and casual believer is brought into knowledge of connecting acquisition of territory with the Kingdom of God. This is beyond every place upon which the soles of your feet shall tread mandate given by God to His nation. It defines and points the believer decidedly in the direction of actual possession of His rightful territory.

Like time, Dr. Ellis is consistent in presenting the truths that will assist the seeker in accomplishing God's will and purpose for his life.

He writes, "The Kingdom of God is not meat and drink; but righteousness, peace and joy in the Holy Ghost. (Romans 14:17) This is God's agenda. His agenda is that we represent Him in the earth. This means we have to act like Him. This means we have to be full of love and compassion and we have to walk right."

Thank God for someone who is not owned by the system and can speak powerfully and declare boldly what God wants of His people.

Dr. Ellis writes further, "The two most important things about a territory are your lifestyle and your concern for people. If these two are not on your agenda then God will not be on your agenda. That is the balance between pulling God so you can get more money. Why should God give you more money so that you can continue to act like a fool? This is God's agenda. He wants to put His Kingdom where ever He can put it. When He saved you, He put the Kingdom in you. When you go to the 7-Eleven ...the Kingdom of God has shown up at the 7-Eleven."

Dr. Ellis pulls you in with every line of this book. WARNING: You will be challenged to grow! It's on every page, so get a warm blanket and get a comfortable position and get ready to change. You will enjoy particularly his impressive manner of backing up his information with revelation. Enjoy!

Dr. Earl Johnson
Pastor Founder
Covenant Life Church Duarte, California

Introduction

At some point in our lives, most of us have found ourselves in a bad situation with circumstances that appeared to be growing worse instead of getting better. We try to "fix" the situation or "change" the circumstance by going to church, seeking godly wisdom from our Pastor, praying, fasting and obtaining godly counsel. All of these things are a good beginning for finding a solution to our problems. However, God has given unto all of His children the potential to overcome every obstacle that confronts them. You will not believe how many people do not realize that the answer to possessing God's plan and journey on the path of destiny for their lives are within them.

<u>Taking Territory: Keys to Possessing Your Promised Land</u> is not just a metaphor for what God desires for you to have. Dr. Jimmie A. Ellis will take you on a compelling journey of biblical proportions and thought provoking insights of "Taking Territory". Dr. Ellis points out one reason in particular that we have a tendency to sidestep after we have been blessed and God has performed miracles in our lives. God blesses us in order for us to be a blessing to someone else. Unfortunately, we do not view things with the same compassion and unselfishness as God would have us to. Oftentimes, we have a selfish and egotistical mindset which makes us believe that the blessings of God are not to be shared. This is what shortchanges the purpose for taking territory and disqualifies us to be a testimony to the world and give the glory back to God.

The central part of this book surveys Old Testament accounts of the people God commanded to take territory and possess land. Some of the Old Testament patriarchs such as Abraham, Moses, Joshua and King David, were each faced with the insurmountable task of defeating nations far greater than themselves in order to take the territory that God had already given into their hands. When you begin to recognize what belongs to you and appropriate it God's way, as did the patriarchs of the Bible, God will empower you to take territory no matter what the test during the process of possessing it. If God strategically waited thirty-eight years to enter the Promised Land so He could remove a generation of doubters and complainers who were a hindrance, we should also wait for His perfect timing in order to claim that which was preordained for us.

Dr. Jimmie A. Ellis, has received revelation from God to communicate to His people the tools for taking territory. By utilizing the tools outlined in this book, God will begin to order your steps and give you clear direction and guidance concerning His Will, His Plan and His Purpose for your life. By reading this book, God will sharpen your discernment on how to recognize adversity, standing in fiery trials, and not allowing devilish distractions and obstacles hinder you from possessing your Promised Land.

What is God personally doing in your life? God is always doing something spectacular and supernatural. God is always moving, progressing, increasing and showing Himself strong in the lives of His people. Even when God is being quiet, everything He is doing in your life is pointing to your future. God wants you to use corresponding actions coupled with His Word in obtaining His plan, destiny and purpose for your life and not just sit complacently and wait for something to happen. Prayer is the miracle for taking territory, but planning is the mechanics.

As you read this book on a consistent and continual basis, God will begin to unfold His plan for you and order your steps on the path of prosperity daily. Everything that you have prayed for and sought God for will begin to manifest in the days to come. Confusion will no longer be a part of your life. Remember, it may take some time for you to gain assurance of what God would have you do, but be patient. Do not faint. Wait on the Lord. Be filled with the knowledge of God's will in all wisdom and spiritual understanding. <u>Taking Territory – Keys to Possessing Your Promised Land</u> will provide you with godly wisdom, instruction, and discernment. As your knowledge increases, your ways shall be established and ordained aright.

CHAPTER ONE

This Territory is Mine!

Rise ye up, take your journey, and pass over the river Arnon: behold, I have given into thine hand Sihon the Amorite, king of Heshbon, and his land: begin to possess it, and contend with him in battle. This day, I will begin to put the dread of thee and the fear of thee upon the nations that are under the whole heaven, who shall hear report of thee, and shall tremble, and be in anguish because of thee. From Aroer, which is by the brink of the river of Arnon, and from the city that is by the river, even unto Gilead, there was not one city too strong for us: the Lord our God delivered all unto us.

DEUTERONOMY 2:24-25, 36

How many of you believe it is time for you to take territory? We are going to learn some things from this story, such as God's will, His way and His wisdom. First and foremost, you must take territory God's way. You cannot do it your way.

The scene of this interesting story takes place while God is talking to Moses. The scripture says:

> Rise ye up, take your journey and pass over to the Arnon River: behold, I have given unto your hand Sihon the Amorite King of Heshbon and his land: begin to possess it with him in the battle.
>
> Then we turned, and went up the way to Bashan: and Og the King of Bashan came out against us, he and all his people, to battle at Edrei.
>
> DEUTERONOMY 3:1

God's Will

Understand that Sihon and Og are partners. God's will was for Moses to take the territory. Why did He tell him at this time to take the territory?

Perfect Timing of God

> Now rise up, said I, and get you over the brook Zered. And we went over the brook Zered. And the space in which we came from Kadesh-barnea, until we were come over the brook Zered, was thirty and eight years; until all the generation of the men of war were wasted out from the among the host, as the Lord sware unto them.
>
> DEUTERONOMY 2:13-14

What happened? First of all, they were out of the will of God and nothing was spoken for 38 years. We do not know what they did during that time. But this was the perfect timing of God because there were no more hindrances.

> For indeed the hand of the Lord was against them, to destroy them from among the host, until they were consumed. So it came to pass, when all the men of war were consumed and dead from among the people, that the Lord spake unto me saying, Thou art to pass over through Ar, the coast of Moab, this day:
> DEUTERONOMY 2:15-18

Again, this was the perfect timing of God. Now, the second generation had been growing up into adulthood. As was stated before, God had removed all the hindrances from them that would have kept them from getting into the Promised Land. This leads into the prophetic timing of God.

The Prophetic Timing of God

> Rise ye up, take your journey, and pass over the river Arnon: behold, I have given into thine hand Sihon the Amorite, king of Heshbon, and his land: begin to possess it, and contend with him in battle.
> DEUTERONOMY 2:24

In Genesis 15, it states the land they were supposed to take belonged to the Canaanites. The Amorites were a part of the Canaanite's land.

> And He said unto Abram, Know of a surety that
> thy seed shall be a stranger in a land that is not
> theirs, and shall serve them; and they shall afflict
> them four hundred years;
> GENESIS 15:13-14

See the prophetic timing of God. God tells Abraham *"your seed is going to be a stranger in a land and that nation whom they shall serve will I judge and after they shall come out with great substance."* (Paraphase)

> And thou shalt go to thy fathers in peace; thou
> shalt be buried in a good old age. But in the fourth
> generation they shall come hither again: for the
> iniquity of the Amorites is not yet full
> GENESIS 15:15-16

God waited for over 400 years for the Amorites to repent; this was God's prophetic timetable. The 400 years were over and it was God's perfect will for Abraham's seed to take the land. Sometimes God makes us wait. There is something prophetic about waiting. Sometimes we cannot take territory until it is time to take it. We may have everything to prepare to take it but it may not be the right time. The way God looks at things goes way beyond the way we look at things. We tend to think when a crime is committed God has to wipe that person out immediately. But, that is not how He does it. God is patient and longsuffering and He will allow the nation to do wickedness until the wickedness becomes so great that the land has to spit out those who are wicked. Let me prove it.

> Moreover thou shalt not lie carnally with thy
> neighbour's wife, to defile thyself with her. And
> thou shalt not let any of thy seed pass through
> the fire to Molech, (Molech was a god of fire and

you worship it by sending your kids through fire.) neither shalt thou profane the name of thy God: I am the Lord. Thou shalt not lie with mankind, as with womankind: it is abomination. Neither shalt thou lie with any beast to defile thyself therewith: neither shall any woman stand before a beast to lie down thereto: it is confusion. Defile not ye yourselves in any of these things: for in all these the nations are defiled which I cast out before you: And the land is defiled: therefore I do visit the iniquity thereof upon it, and the land itself vomiteth out her inhabitants.

LEVITICUS 18:20-25

The timing for Moses to take the territory was right because the Amorites had sinned so badly. It was not time for Israelites to relax and have a good time. It was just perfect timing. It is God's prophetic timetable for us to take the land. Now is the time for us to claim our houses. Do you think that the housing market is going crazy right now without a reason? What people do not understand is that waiting does not mean to do nothing. No, waiting means that something is about to happen. While Israel was sitting in the wilderness it appeared to be a curse, but God was operating behind the scenes and the prophetic timetable was moving forward. You would be surprised what God is doing while you are waiting. Waiting time is not lost time. Waiting time is fulfillment time. You will have to trust God during the waiting period. He works everything out according to the counsel of His own will. It is a perfect time! It is a prophetic time for us to take territory. One thing I love about God is that He will tell you which territory to take and this leads to my next point.

You Are Not Supposed to Take a Territory That is Not Yours

> God marked out the boundaries which is from
> the brink of Arnon from the city that is by the
> river even unto Gilead…even unto Gilead, there
> was not one city too strong for us: the Lord our
> God delivered all unto us: Only unto the land
> of the children of Ammon thou camest not, nor
> unto any place of the river Jabbok, nor unto
> the cities in the mountains, nor unto whatso-
> ever the Lord our God forbad us.
> DEUTERONOMY 2:36-37

Now, God is marking the boundaries of what they are supposed to take and how far they are supposed to take it.

There were certain areas surrounding the territory that they
were not supposed to take. However, the territory that God tells
us to possess is so important that if we start trespassing into
territory that He did not tell us to take, He will not be with us.
The anointing will not be there and we will be defeated.

> And when thou comest nigh over against the chil-
> dren of Ammon, distress them not, nor meddle with
> them: for I will not give thee of the land of the chil-
> dren of Ammon any possession; because I have given
> it unto the children of Lot for a possession.
> DEUTERONOMY 2:19

Sometimes we cannot take a territory because it belongs to
someone else. How do you know when you are trespassing into
someone else's territory? Here are a few ways you can tell.

1. When you are trying to be something that you are not.

We trespass into someone else's territory when we try to emulate them. There is enough of God's personality in us to know that we have the right territory. The world is extremely big and if we just practice being ourselves, we will attract the kinds of people who are ordained by God to help us. It is only when we pry into someone else's territory that we start to act like them. There are billions of people in this world. This is one reason why I do not stress over people leaving my church. Admittedly, I do not like it, but I do not stress over it because God has plenty of people in this world. Do not worry when people leave you. Sometimes new people cannot come into your life until the old people are gone. Preachers, do not try to teach if that is not your gifting. You have your own territory and you have the personality to fit that territory. For instance, if somebody doesn't like the way you communicate, then it was not predetermined for them to link with your territory. Do not change your personality in order to please someone else. Avoid those who try to be a puppet master in your life. Stay away from people who have a controlling spirit because they are trying to change you into something that you are not. Retain the power to say 'yes' or 'no'. I remember an old secular song that says, "I just want to thank you for letting me be myself". If something is being communicated that you don't like, you are entitled to your own opinion.

2. Trying to do something that you are not anointed to do.

Many people neglect their own territory because they are trying to do something that God never told them to do. We can understand why certain churches have the same number of people and it remains that way for years. Whenever God gives a fruit, it is because there is a root. How do you know you're gifted? You are gifted when someone can follow you without being coerced.

If you can sing, people will hear the power of your voice. There will be something unique in the way you sing. You do not have to sing or sound like another person; you will still gain vast reception because you are anointed in that area. It is silly to try to do something that you are not anointed to do.

3. You invade a wrong territory when you try to take something without a word from God.

Years ago there was a member of my church who believed he could do things better than I. He proclaimed "I can do what Bishop does and I can do it better." When I heard about it I had a meeting with him. I could see that he "was" called to preach, but not at that time. He was still a child in the Spirit. But, since he believed that he was ready, I released him into ministry. It was very difficult for me to do this because I know that when a person doesn't realize that they are "not" yet ready to do something, they feel that you are trying to control them. We need to have enough Holy Ghost inside of us for when someone tells us 'no,' we will know it is for our good. No is one word in particular that people do not like to hear, but it is sometimes more of a blessing than a curse. That is why we should wait.

When people are patting us on our back and saying "you are all that," it may go to our head and we may not want to wait. As a pastor, I knew what was best for him. He just was not ready. I said, "We are going to send you out," and we sent him out. I did not publicize the situation because I wanted to cover him. He moved to another state and founded his church. There were no congregants for three months. The only parishioners were his wife and children. Again, just because you see someone doing something doesn't mean you are prepared to do it as well. Some of us are better at certain tasks than others, but that is because of the anointing. When you see someone performing a task it will always appear easy to you, but keep in mind the anointing is hiding all of the sweat involved. Many believe that it is easy for me to do what I do, but that's because they don't see the blood, sweat, and tears I've invested. Do not try to walk in another person's territory because there is enough territory for everyone. I repeat, stay in your own territory.

4. You must have God's will for your territory.

There are two reasons for this. First, you must live within the parameters of God's will in order to know your territory. This will produce confidence. When God tells you to go and possess something, it will build confidence in your spirit. It is one thing for people to say you can do a particular thing, but it is entirely different when God says, "You can do it." When God tells you to go and take the land, you will have the confidence to proceed and conquer. Second, you need to know the will of God. Just because God says the land is yours doesn't mean there won't be problems.

Satan will throw everything at you and the only thing that will help you stand is a Word from God. When God tells you that you can take territory, it will give you the strength to endure disappointments, setbacks or any other hindrances that comes your way. The only thing that will help you to stand in the midst of hell is what God told you to do.

> ...Begin to possess it, and contend with him in battle.
> DEUTERONOMY 2:24B

It was the will of God for Moses to take the territory, but God's way of taking it was to vigorously fight for it. In other words, we may have a battle on our hands. What we see in the realm of the Spirit, will still have to be won within the confines of the natural. It is alright to rejoice about having clear direction, but just because we see it in the Spirit doesn't guarantee that it is going to be easy. Sometimes God stirs up conflict. God is letting you know that your territory is in the battle.

Moses said, And I sent messengers out of the wilderness of Kedemoth unto Sihon king of Heshbon with words of peace, saying, let me pass through thy land: I will go along by the high way, I will neither turn unto the right hand nor to the left. Thou shalt sell me meat for money, that I may eat; and give me water for money, that I may drink: only I will pass through on my feet; (As the children of Esau which dwell in Seir, and the Moabites which dwell in Ar, did unto me;) until I shall pass over Jordan into the land which the Lord our God giveth us. But Sihon king of Heshbon would not let us pass by him: for the Lord thy God hardened his spirit, and made his heart obstinate, that he might deliver him into thy hand, as appeareth this day.

DEUTERONOMY 2:26-30

Moses is trying to be a peacemaker by explaining that they would not be able to cross the Jordan without going through the man's land. God stirs the man's heart to say, "We are not going to let you pass." We don't want to believe that God does these kinds of things, but Jesus was led by the Spirit into the wilderness to be tested by the devil. Sometimes God's way is not positive. Sometimes God's way seems ridiculous, but God is up to something here.

Sihon, the King of Hesbon would not let him pass. For the Lord your God hardened his spirit and made his heart stubborn that he might deliver him into thy hands as it appears unto this day. And the Lord said unto me, Behold, I have begun to give Sihon his land before you. Begin to possess that you may inherit his land.

DEUTERONOMY 2:30-31

You cannot receive a word from God and be done with it. You have to take that word and face the enemy with it. You must face the challenge. Your territory will be bigger than you. That is what makes God's vision a vision. If the vision is small it is not from God. God will give you a vision that is bigger than you are because He wants to stretch you. God is not a kindergarten God. He is a college God. We want to hear what God is saying, but we don't want to act upon it. You hear good instructions about taking territory, but you develop an attitude of hoping something will happen out of the clear blue. By doing this you refuse to face your giants. It doesn't work that way.

> And because he loved thy fathers, therefore he chose their seed after them, and brought thee out in his sight with his mighty power out of Egypt; To drive out nations from before thee greater and mightier than thou art, to bring thee in, to give thee their land for an in-heritance, as it is this day.
> DEUTERONOMY 4:37-38

> When the Lord thy God shall bring thee into the land whither thou goest to possess it, and hath cast out many nations before thee, the Hittites, and the Girgashites, and the Amorites, and the Canaanites, and the Perizzites, and the Hivites, and the Jebusites, seven nations greater and mightier than thou;
> DEUTERONOMY 7:1

The vision was for them to take the land, but how were they going to take the land when they were a tiny nation going against nations mightier than they?

> Hear, O Israel: Thou art to pass over Jordan this day, to go in to possess nations greater and mightier than thyself, cities great and fenced up to heaven,
>
> DEUTERONOMY 9:1

He is talking about giants in the land.

> A people great and tall, the children of the Anakims, whom thou knowest, and of whom thou hast heard say, Who can stand before the children of Anak! Understand therefore this day, that the Lord thy God is he which goeth over before thee; as a consuming fire he shall destroy them, and he shall bring them down before thy face: so shalt thou drive them out, and destroy them quickly, as the Lord hath said unto thee.
>
> DEUTERONOMY 9:2-3

Yes, God will do the work, but you have to show up. God is saying, "I am going to perform the miracle, but you have to be available." Don't be involved with something else when God shows up. Face the enemy!!! Let the enemy know that even though you are scared, you are confident because God told you to do it. God is saying, "I cannot destroy the enemy if you do not get in the enemy's face." Goliath would never have been defeated had David stayed with the sheep. He had to face Goliath! You cannot leave it up to others to get the job done. You have to have some backbone. You must be confident and you must have courage.

What territory has God told you to take that is bigger than you? What particular thing has God told you to take? I am not talking about making a phone call to place an order. What I am asking is what territory has God given you that is so big that it will cause you to fall on your knees? That is what God wants you to do. He wants you to seek Him so He can be first in your life and show you how big He is.

The problem with some people is that they are too lazy. God is trying to shake the laziness out of you. When someone like Bill Cosby or President Barack Obama tells us about it, we tend to get upset and we want to remain complacent. It is amazing how other nations can come to America and possess territory. It is amazing how Asians can share one room with ten relatives. But they don't mind the challenge of taking territory because they have the mentality that they can do it together.

We, as African Americans, do not have that mentality. The Asians suffer so they can reign. Within 10 years they prosper because they are not lazy people. They are industrious. They say to one another, you take this part and I'll take that part.

They don't put their parents in nursing homes. They take care of them until they die because it is part of their culture. They walk with their parents and will not throw them away after they become wealthy. They value their parents' wisdom.

African Americans must move beyond just listening to good preaching and going back to our huts and remaining in our comfort zone. We don't have dreams or visions!! All we have is good preaching. You need more than good preaching to take territory. You need courage and a plan. You must let the enemy know that you are not afraid of him. And even if you are scared, do not let your enemy know it. When the children of Israel went down to the Red Sea, Moses told the people not to fear; but he himself was as scared as ever. You know what God told him to do? Use the rod, the same rod that had turned water into blood and caused frogs to come forth. This is the Word of the Lord: Use your rod! It's taken you this far. God says, "Take the rod and stretch it out over the waters." God is pushing you toward a negative circumstance so you can change the situation.

Our church is located in Southwest Philadelphia, one of the worst areas in the city when it comes to crime. As people of God, we cannot stick our heads in the sand. We are here to help bring about change. Therefore change your territory! Many families have endured poverty for years. Married couples have failed, family members have remained sick, and singles have refused to get married. But when God places the anointing on your life, it makes a difference and reverses the curse that has plagued your family. Wake up! Look at what you have. Stop shouting over power you refuse to use.

CHAPTER TWO

Joshua's Five Secrets

On that day, the Lord magnified Joshua in the sight of all Israel; and they feared him, as they feared [respected] Moses all the days of his life.

JOSHUA 4:14

And the Lord gave unto Israel all the land which he sware to give unto their fathers; and they possessed it, and dwelt therein. And the Lord gave them rest round about, according to all that he sware unto their fathers: and there stood not a man of all their enemies before them; the Lord delivered all their enemies into their hand. There failed not aught of any good thing which the Lord had spoken unto the house of Israel; all came to pass.

JOSHUA 21:43-45

If ever there was one who knew how to take territory, it was Joshua. Joshua picked up the mantle from Moses and led Israel into their Promised Land in seven and a half years. Joshua was impressive because he'd fought and defeated thirty-one nations.

David was also able to take territory. The Bible says that David took Zion and Jerusalem. I knew David was awesome on the battlefield, but I would not have thought that about Joshua. David was such a fierce warrior that God said, "You cannot build me a house because your hands are too bloody." You are waiting for someone to give you your territory, but you have to take it.

> And these are the kings of the country which Joshua and the children of Israel smote on this side Jordan on the west, from Baalgad in the valley of Lebanon even unto the mount Halak, that goeth up to Seir; which Joshua gave unto the tribes of Israel for a possession according to their divisions;
> JOSHUA 12:7

In Chapter One, we talked about Sihon and Og, the cities on the east of Jordan. Now, Joshua's job is to conquer the ones on the west.

> In the mountains, and in the valleys, and in the plains, and in the springs, and in the wilderness, and in the south country; the Hittites, the Amorites, and the Canaanites, the Perizzites, the Hivites, and the Jebusites: The king of Jericho, one; the king of Ai, which is beside Bethel, one; The king of Tirzah one; all the kings thirty and one.
> JOSHUA 12:8-9, 24

Even though God said the land is yours, there is still work to be done. Joshua went on to defeat thirty-one nations and took their land.

Now, let us discuss **Joshua's Five Success Secrets**. They all begin with the letter "F".

Secret #1: Joshua Had a FATHER

Joshua knew how to take territory because he had someone in his life as an example – His Spiritual Father, Moses.

Many times we want our father's clothes, cars, and money but there is something else more valuable. We need our father's spirit. A father is someone who is seasoned enough to show us the ropes. A father has territory. A father can say, "This is my turf and I am going to pass it on to you." He is not afraid to give you information because he is not intimidated by you. He can tell you what you need to know and then go about his business. Fathers are not bothered by us because they do not need us to feel validated. That just disqualified half of the mentors. You cannot be a father (or mother) in the gospel and not be seasoned. Do not tell me to follow you when I haven't seen fruit of your labor.

Make this a year where you are going to connect with someone who already knows the ropes and not someone who is still trying to find them. Stop hanging around people who lie! I am talking about people who want you to think that they have something. Just because somebody is wearing a sharp suit does not mean they have money! Who is your example?

How can you take new territory when you don't even know how to do it? It is an unchanging principle. Joshua had a father to teach him.

Do you know why Jesus was so successful? He had a Father. Each of us needs a father (or a mother) who is experienced in spiritual matters. They do not have to keep telling us what they possess. If someone is a father, we can see it because they have children. Who is a father and who is a mother? A father or a mother is someone who shows you the ropes. That is the reason you connect with them. It is not for them to become your friend. In some cases, friendships may form, but not at the beginning. They have the territory to prove it. My spiritual father, Bishop Don Meares, has territory. I am not referring to his money, but his wisdom. He has it and I recognized it the first time we met.

For those of you who do not have someone to teach you, pray and ask God to send you someone. Do not submit to someone because they are politicking for you to follow them. We have turned the Kingdom of God into a political show. Many will ask, "Will you follow me?" People who do that are insecure within themselves. That is not the right spirit. If we just mind our business, the right person will connect with us.

> Then answered Jesus and said unto them, Verily, verily, I say unto you, The Son can do nothing of himself, but what he seeth the Father do: for what things soever he doeth, these also doeth the Son likewise.
>
> JOHN 5:19

We must grasp the spirit of the person who is leading us. We are totally ignorant of where God wants to take us and that is why we are confused right now. We know God gave us the territory, but who is the person to lead us? God is not going to meet us at 7:00 every morning and give us instructions. He has told us enough so when we meet the person, we will know in our spirit that they are the one to lead us.

> As the Lord commanded Moses his servant, so did Moses command Joshua, and so did Joshua; he left nothing undone of all that the Lord commanded Moses.
>
> JOSHUA 11:15

> So Joshua took the whole land, according to all that
> the Lord said unto Moses; and Joshua gave it for an
> inheritance unto Israel according to their divisions
> by their tribes. And the land rested from war.
>   JOSHUA 11:23

A few years ago people said, "We are the Joshua Generation; we don't need Moses." People were saying that all over the country. Don't get it twisted. There would not be a Joshua had there not been a Moses.

Secret #2: Joshua FOLLOWED

Joshua did not go around announcing that Moses was his father. He had a father by following Moses. Joshua connected with his father to become his servant, not his buddy. He related to him as a servant.

If you want to know how to conquer, you have to learn how to follow. This means keeping our mouth closed and opening it only to ask questions. You need your mentor to give you the essence of his spirit. We don't have to talk about our credentials. We should act as if we don't have any.

I have my Dad's spirit because when I am talking to him, I do not tell him what I am doing until he asks me. I ask questions. I am not there to waste his time by saying, "Let us party and hang out." We should keep our mouths shut until we learn how to ask questions. When we talk to our mentors, we shouldn't dominate the conversation because our mentor is not there for us to give him an interview. We must listen to our mentors because we do not know how to take territory. Be honest and humble yourself. You do not know how to take territory so listen and learn. We don't have to move in with them, just learn to listen.

> And it came to pass, as Moses entered into the tabernacle, the cloudy pillar descended, and stood at the door of the tabernacle, and the Lord talked with Moses. And all the people saw the cloudy pillar stand at the tabernacle door: and all the people rose up and worshipped, every man in his tent door. And the Lord spake unto Moses face to face, as a man speaketh unto his friend. And he turned again into the camp: but his ser-vant Joshua, the son of Nun, a young man, departed not out of the tabernacle.
>
> EXODUS 33:9-11

How did the disciples transition from discipleship to apostleship? By following the leader. How did the apostles learn to lay hands on the sick and raise the dead? They were not born with that power. Jesus showed them how to do it. They were humble enough to receive it. This principle not only works in the church but in other occupations and relationships as well.

The best thing that a single woman could ever do for herself is connect with a married woman who has been married for about ten years or more. Talk to her and tell her you have some questions about marriage and that you believe you are going to be married one day. Stop discussing marriage issues with single women. There are certain things about marriage that single people will never know. Get under a solid married person who does not argue with their mate all the time. Tell them you want to know how they were able to stay with that man when his bad side manifested. Ask them how they reacted in an argument.

Single men, if you want to get married, interact with a man who has a solid marriage, and ask questions. We must humble ourselves. Some of us think we know everything. How can you know everything when you are on your third or fourth marriage? What we don't understand is that there is a cycle going on in your life. You should have a mentor for whatever you want to be in life. Humble yourself and follow that person's instructions. I do not mean for you to follow him or her home, I mean follow their instructions.

Why can't you keep money? You get a refund check for thousands of dollars and by the end of the month it is all gone. Perhaps, you do not want to face the fact that you need help. Even at the age of 12, Jesus was wise enough to know that He needed doctors and lawyers! We do not know everything. The more territory we take, the more information we will need. Would you like to own a home? Do you know how to go about purchasing one? If we do not know how to buy a house, we need to connect with someone who does. Link up with someone who is prosperous.

In order to keep poverty away from us we have to read and sit under someone with wisdom, knowledge and understanding. We have to give that person information on our spending habits, but we don't want to do that. If we don't listen, we will be in the same predicament next year. As a pastor I preach the same thing different ways and I'd like to look back and see that someone transitioned from poverty to wealth because they picked up my spirit.

How do you get rid of spirits? We can lay hands on you and cast out a spirit; but how do you keep the spirit away? You do not get rid of spirits just by casting them out. In order to keep them away from you, you need wisdom. You must fill your soul with knowledge.

> Be not slothful, but be followers of them who
> through faith and patience inherit the promises.
> HEBREWS 6:12

Being a follower pays off. Information pays off. Wisdom pays off.

And Moses spake unto the Lord, saying, Let the
Lord, the God of the spirits of all flesh, set a man
over the congregation, Which may go out before
them, and which may go in before them, and
which may lead them out, and which may bring
them in; that the congregation of the Lord be not
as sheep which have no shepherd. And the Lord
said unto Moses, Take thee Joshua the son of Nun,
a man in whom is the spirit, and lay thine hand
upon him; And set him before Eleazar the priest,
and before all the congregation; and give him a
charge in their sight. And thou shalt put some of
thine honour upon him, that all the congregation
of the children of Israel may be obedient.
NUMBERS 27:15-20

It pays to follow because when we follow, we get a mantle.
Do you know what pastors, preachers and people like Donald
Trump and Oprah are looking for? They are looking for somebody to pass their honor to. When it is time for you to die, you
want to die empty. Donald Trump has "The Apprentice" on
television because he wants to help people through what he
knows. He wants to pass his spirit on to someone else.

That is the good thing about Elijah. When Elijah went to
heaven, he left the mantle. He went to heaven but he left behind his principles. God does not want your principles to go to
heaven; He wants your principles to go to someone else. When
Jesus went on to heaven, what happened? 120 people caught
His spirit. He told 500 people to meet Him but only 120 of
them obeyed. That goes to show you how many people really
obey the words of a mentor.

Secret #3: Joshua was a FIGHTER

God is trying to tell us that it is time to fight and put our actions behind our words. Joshua was a fighter. Let this be a year that we are going to fight.

> Then came Amalek, and fought with Israel in Rephidim. And Moses said unto Joshua, Choose us out men, and go out, fight with Amalek: tomorrow I will stand on the top of the hill with the rod of God in mine hand.
> EXODUS 17:8

Moses directed Joshua to fight with Amalek because this fight was practice for him to become the next leader. Joshua fought with Amalek and won. God wanted Joshua to fight because it was teaching him how to take territory.

If we do not get up to do something, our calling will be ineffective. People do not call us by our title because it sounds pretty. They call us by our title based on what we do.

> And Joshua discomfited Amalek and his people with the edge of the sword. And the Lord said unto Moses, Write this for a memorial in a book, and rehearse it in the ears of Joshua: for I will utterly put out the remembrance of Amalek from under heaven.
> EXODUS 17:13-14

When Moses told Joshua to do things Joshua could not understand why he was chosen to do it. It is because a mentor knows how to stretch you to prepare you.

God did not tell Joshua anything. He told Moses to write the war in a book and start talking about it to Joshua. Communicate and rehearse it in his ears. Make him go to war. In other words, make him carry a briefcase. Make him go to church on Wednesday nights. Make him go to church on Sunday. Make him come here early and be the last one to leave. For all of us who want to be the president of a corporation, we need to be the first one there and the last one to leave.

Joshua was a fighter. He learned by practice that you fight until you win. He saw Moses fight until he won. That is what we need to see, people who take a stand and do not quit every five minutes.

> Then said Joshua, Open the mouth of the cave, and bring out those five kings unto me out of the cave. And they did so, and brought forth those five kings unto him out of the cave, the king of Jerusalem, the king of Hebron, the king of Jarmuth, the king of Lachish, and the king of Eglon. And it came to pass, when they brought out those kings unto Joshua, that Joshua called for all the men of Israel, and said unto the captains of the men of war which went with him, come near, put your feet upon the necks of these kings. And they came near, and put their feet upon the necks of them. And Joshua said unto them, Fear not, nor be dismayed, be strong and of good courage: for thus shall the Lord do to all your enemies against whom ye fight. And afterward Joshua smote them, and slew them, and hanged them on five trees: and they were hanging upon the trees until the evening.
>
> JOSHUA 10:22-26

> So Joshua took the whole land, according to all that the Lord said unto Moses; and Joshua gave it for an inheritance unto Israel according to their divisions by their tribes. And the land rested from war.
>
> JOSHUA 11:23

Secret #4: Joshua had FAITH

If we are going to take territory, we must have faith.

> And all the congregation lifted up their voice, and cried; and the people wept that night. And all the children of Israel murmured against Moses and against Aaron: and the whole congregation said unto them, Would God that we had died in the land of Egypt! or would God we had died in this wilderness! And wherefore hath the Lord brought us unto this land, to fall by the sword, that our wives and our children should be a prey? Were it not better for us to return into Egypt? And they said one to another, Let us make a captain, and let us return into Egypt. Then Moses and Aaron fell on their faces before all the assembly of the congregation of the children of Israel. And Joshua the son of Nun, and Caleb the son of Jephunneh, which were of them that searched the land, rent their clothes: And they spake unto all the company of the children of Israel, saying, The land, which we passed through to search it, is an exceeding good land. If the Lord delight in us, then he will bring us into this land, and give it us; a land which floweth with milk and honey. Only rebel not ye against the Lord, neither fear ye the people of the land; for they are bread for us: their defence is departed from them, and the Lord is with us: fear them not.
>
> NUMBERS 14:1-9

Caleb had discernment. God was telling them to move on. God was telling them that there are better things for them. No, do not talk about going back to the wilderness.

Joshua and Caleb said, "Do not rebel against the Lord and do not fear the people. They are bread for us and their defense has departed." Notice what they said. They were looking at it from the eyes of God. If we want to take territory, we have to look at it from the eyes of God. You may not have the money, but look at it from the eyes of God. If God told you that you can take it, say "God told me to take it." "We can do it." "Let us search for money." "Let us look for it." "If God says we can have the house, Let us look for the house." If you want to go back to school go onto the internet and search for grants.

My grandmother taught me years ago that if I made one step God would take two. She was saying if I made an effort, then God would match my effort.

Just looking at ESPN and soap operas will not help us. Joshua had faith. How did he get the faith? He hung around Moses. Moses had the faith. That is why we need to come to church because when we lose faith it is good to be around others who have it.

Secret #5: Joshua had a FRIEND

> Surely they shall not see the land which I sware
> unto their fathers, neither shall any of them that
> provoked me see it: But my servant Caleb, because
> he had another spirit with him, and hath followed
> me fully, him will I bring into the land whereinto
> he went; and his seed shall possess it.
> NUMBERS 14:23-24

Most people say we should hook up with people who are not like us. Well, I disagree. Yes, we need to get with someone who is different from us but only when we possess the land. Until we can possess the land, we need to have someone with us that has just as much fire as we do.

How silly is it for someone who is a "go-getter" by personality to be connected with somebody who is passive when you are talking about preparing for tomorrow and the person you are connected to is lazy about it. We do not need somebody that is opposite of us. We need somebody like us. Why? Because opposites attract but they do not last! Let God hook you up with somebody that has a similar spirit. You like to read, I like to read. You like cars, I like cars. Do you know that hooking up with someone that has the wrong spirit will slow down your vision?

Some married people are discouraged because they married a person with the wrong spirit. I do not mean that they are demon possessed, but they cannot flow with your goals. They are not wired that way. Don't think that because you married that person that you can change them. Some people are suffering right now for this very reason. When we are single, we can put our relationships on hold until we accomplish our individual goals. Why? If we hook up with someone that does not believe in our dreams, we will be held back for at least five years.

We've been taught that opposites attract. After living for a while, I do not agree with that at all. Why do movie stars marry movie stars? Why do doctors marry doctors? It is because they understand the flow. If I get married one day, I have to marry someone that likes ministry. Why should I marry someone who is fine and shaped like a coca-cola bottle and cannot live out her purpose? We are looking for the most attractive, and the sexiest person. But the issue is whenever we want to do something, they do not want us to do it. They start blocking our plans because we are staying out too long. They want us to stay home with them, kissing on them. If I can do my vision, I can buy you a house and we can have romance all of the time. If you let me do my dream, we can fly the friendly skies. If you let me do my dream, we do not have to fuss over the car. You will have a car and I will have a car. Get somebody like you. You do not have to agree with me. If you want somebody opposite, that is on you but I want somebody like me. When you get somebody like you, there is less explaining. If you are in the business, you need to hook up with someone that likes music so when you are in the studio all night, they will not think of you as being disloyal.

As I said before, doctors marry doctors, because doctors know that they have to give their lives to school. So, if you go to school and the person you are hooking up with goes to school, there is less explanation. If I marry someone that is in ministry I will not have to explain to her why I will not take her out to dinner after service. She will know that I am tired.

If you are the type of person that is on fire in your personality, find someone that is on fire in their personality. You may say, "If the two people are on fire both of them will burn out". That will only make their love grow deeper. You will not go to divorce court. Get someone that is on fire like you are. This is what made Joshua last.

Let me show you how important this was to Joshua. This was important to Joshua because what you do not realize is that Joshua had to postpone his vision for 40 years. He had to postpone his vision because the other ten spies could not believe.

What do you do when you have to wait 40 years because of something that is not your fault? What do you do when you have to delay your dream based on the wrong people? Thank God that while Joshua was waiting for 40 years, he could look over and see Caleb. He could look over and say, "Caleb are you waiting? I am waiting too. Do you still believe God? I still believe God!"

For those who are in college, get with another student that wants to graduate so that when you get discouraged, you can communicate your concerns with them and they can encourage you not to quit! I read a book about four guys who hung out with each other as kids and decided to go to college together. They all graduated as doctors. They were all African-American. When the going got tough and some of them ran out of money, they encouraged one another because they all had the hidden ingredients called fire and passion. You have to hook up with a person that already has it. Passion has to be birthed on the inside of you. Just because you marry someone does not mean that they will have passion. Passion comes out in the way you walk. Passion comes out in the way you talk. Passion comes out in the way you solve problems.

> Then the children of Judah came unto Joshua in Gilgal: and Caleb the son of Jephunneh the Kenezite said unto him, Thou knowest the thing that the Lord said unto Moses the man of God concerning me and thee in Kadeshbarnea. Forty years old was I when Moses the servant of the Lord sent me from Kadeshbarnea to spy out the land; and I brought him word again as it was in mine heart. Nevertheless my brethren that went up with me made the heart of the people melt: but I wholly followed the Lord my God. And Moses sware on that day, saying, Surely the land whereon thy feet have trodden shall be thine inheritance, and thy children's for ever, because thou hast wholly followed the Lord my God. And now, behold, the Lord hath kept me alive, as he said, these forty and five years, even since the Lord spake this word unto Moses, while the children of Is-rael wandered in the wilderness: and now, lo, I am this day fourscore and five years old (85 years old). As yet I am as strong this day as I was in the day that Moses sent me: as my strength was then, even so is my strength now, for war, both to go out, and to come in.
>
> JOSHUA 14:6-11

Passion was in Joshua's personality. You cannot just lay hands and give somebody that. Joshua hooked up with the right person. If you want to take your territory, find that somebody that wants to take territory too so when you are down and out, they can encourage you.

CHAPTER THREE

Too Selfish to Help Someone Else

Now the Lord had said unto Abram, Get thee out of thy country, and from thy kindred, and from they father's house, unto a land that I will shew thee: and I will make of thee a great nation, and I will bless thee, and make thy name great; and thou shalt be a blessing:

GENESIS 12:1-2

A territorial trap you have to be aware of is being too selfish to help someone else. The text tells us very clearly that God had territory for Abraham. God told Abraham to get out of his land and go to a land that He had purposed for him. Then He told him three things and said if Abraham did them, He would make of him a great nation. The first thing that God said was He would bless Abraham and make his name great. In other words, Abraham's name will never die, which it has not all these thousands of years. Notice what He said at the end of the verse: "You shall be a blessing." God's promises to Abraham were,

1) He would give Abraham the land
2) He would bless him in the land
3) He would make him a blessing to others

There is a connection between possessing the land and being a blessing. He said if you be a blessing, I will bless them that bless you. God told me something. He said, "Son, I am looking for a lover." He is looking for somebody who wants to be a blessing to someone else.

Why does God want us to be a blessing? He said, first of all, Abraham, when I bless you and you turn around to bless someone else, I am going to move you from being a person to becoming a partner. You see, in this country, we are used to being individualistic. You have SELF and ME Magazines. (Yes, there is a ME Magazine.) But God is trying to get Abraham to go from me to we. He wants to move you from being blessed in your personhood to being blessed as a partner. God does not want you to be blessed and it is only for you, your family or your friends. One of the reasons why He wants to give you more is to bless more people. It does not start when you get the territory; it starts with the territory that you are on already. I do not think you know how important this is to God, because, after all, when He said you, He was not concerned for only you. He placed you in a community with other people. He placed you in a body of believers.

In Genesis 14, Lot was kidnapped when a war broke out in his territory.

> And they took all the goods of Sodom and
> Gomorrah, and all their victuals, and went their
> way. And they took lot, Abram's brother's son,

who dwelt in Sodom, and his goods, and departed. And there came one that had escaped, and told Abram the Hebrew; for he dwelt in the plain of Mamre the Amorite, brother of Eshcol, and brother of Aner: and these were confederate with Abram. And when Abram heard that his brother was taken captive, he armed his trained servants, born in his own house, three hundred and eighteen, and pursued them unto Dan. And he divided himself against them, he and his servants, by night, and smote them, and pursued them unto Hobah, which is on the left hand of Damascus.

GENESIS 14:11-15

Look at the heart of Abraham. Even though they were separated Abraham was willing to fight on Lot's behalf. The Bible is very unique. It says in Genesis 14:14 "…when Abraham heard that his brother was taken captive." If you know your Bible, you know that Lot is not Abraham's brother – he is his nephew. But when we are connected to someone in the spirit, it does not matter whether he is Abraham's nephew. You are not related by natural blood. We are related by spiritual blood and when something happens to our brother (or sister) in Christ, we are supposed to take our territory and help our brother who has been taken captive. We do not see that very often because we are selfish. The closer we get to the coming of the Lord, the more selfish we become. This is why we must be careful as believers. We cannot copy success from the world. The world has taken our principles and become successful by using them. The world even knows how to give. That is why we must be the example and be a blessing. In case you don't believe that, look what it says in Matthew 24.

For nation shall rise against nation, and kingdom against kingdom: and there shall be famines, and pestilences, and earthquakes, in divers places. All

these are the beginning of sorrows. Then shall they
deliver you up to be afflicted, and shall kill you:
and ye shall be hated of all nations for my name's
sake. And then shall many be offended, and shall
betray one another, and shall hate one another.
MATTHEW 24:7-10

It is hard to find a good friend these days. You tell someone
today that your toe hurts and by the time you hear it again, it is
your hand that was hurting. People cannot even tell the story
correctly.

...and shall betray one another and you shall hate
one another. And many false prophets shall arise
and deceive many. And because iniquity shall
abound, the love of many shall wax cold.
MATTHEW 24:10B-12

God is not talking about the world in this verse. He is talking about believers. He goes on to say the love of many shall
grow cold. The word love means agape. No, you do not wake
up not loving; you grow into not loving.

This know also, that in the last days perilous times
shall come. For men shall be lovers of their own
selves, covetous, boasters, proud, blasphemers,
disobedient to parents, unthankful, unholy,
2 TIMOTHY 3:1-2

Selfishness is the first item listed. Whenever you are selfish
you are bound to display the following characteristics:
covetous-ness, being boastful, pride, blasphemous, disobedient
to parents (you do not respect their authority), unthankful and
unholy. How many of you know that selfishness is not a part of
God's agenda? What I am saying is very vital. The two things

that you always have to stay on top of are: 1) your lifestyle must always represent God; and 2) you must be willing to help others. Once you start displaying selfish behavior, you will begin to cut off your own bless-ing. Do you understand that there are some people who will never come inside a church but your lifestyle is an example of the church to them? Let me tell you three things that happen when you bless someone else.

1. You reproduce what God did for you.

As you receive from God, you become like God when you give to someone else. When God blesses you through the heart of an individual, you ought to turn around and be a blessing to another person.

2. You re-establish unity and connection.

It was God's will that Abraham and Lot be separated. When Abraham went back to help Lot, it re-established connection. Ladies and gentlemen, you are not connected just because you tell your neighbor "I love you." It is when you give of yourself. I do not assume nowadays that people are givers because people are basically selfish. For example, the divorce rate would not be so high if husbands and wives gave more of themselves to each other. Stop waiting for someone to come to ask us for help and be the first to make the step towards them because God is our source.

We should be concerned about how we treat each other. God does not see things like we do. We think we are blessed because we know the Word of God. God is saying we can know the Word all we want, but there has to be demonstration of the Word that we study. God would rather we know one scripture, such as *The Lord is my shepherd I shall not want* (Psalm 23:1) and be a blessing to someone, than for us to know all 66 books of the Bible and not speak to people. Let me get something straight; ministry is people. Ministry means getting dirty. Ministry means taking a risk. Every time we love, we take a risk. Every time we say, "Praise God" to someone, we take a risk because we may not get a response.

Do you know why we find it hard to love? It is because we like to play it safe. Do you want to know what God said to me recently? He reminded me that when He died on that cross He took a risk. I know He took a risk, because some of the people He died for still do not believe in Him. But this does not stop God from loving them. Do not let our love stop because other people do not receive it. Do not clog up your well because other people do not want to drink your water. Jesus said, *"I came to my own and my own did not receive me." But for those who did, to them He gave power to become the sons of God.* (Paraphrase John 1:7)

For those of you that have gotten divorced, your life is not over because your mate left you. God is making another Adam, or another Eve. I know the divorce cut you to your heart, but ask God to heal you and keep right on moving. If they left you, turn the page and start a new chapter in your life. Do not stop being friendly because some friends were phony. This is exactly what the devil wants you to do. He wants you to shut down. God has too much for you to do and you are too gifted to stay isolated. Kiss them good-bye. This is a brand new day! Say, "I have new territory, new friends and a new attitude." Go get a new dress. Go get a new pair of shoes. Go get a new suit because you have a new attitude. Do not stop loving. If you stop loving, you will cut off your blessing. Remember, there are six billion people in this world, someone will accept you for who you are.

3. You replenish your own soul.

When you love people and give of yourself, it makes you feel good to know that you were a part of their solution. Selfish people are not happy people. They look for wrong in you because they are not happy with themselves. The key to happiness is for you to give yourself away. If you would just give yourself away, God would replenish you with more. It is wonderful to be able to say, "God used me. Wow, someone did not kill himself or herself because God used me. Someone's needs were met because God used me." When was the last time you helped someone? These are very practical principles for all of you who are seeking territory, God is looking for lovers. I am a living witness that when you reach out to help people, God will give you more.

David said, "I have b*een young, and now am old; yet have I not seen the righteous forsaken, nor His seed begging bread."* (Paraphrase Psalms 37:25) David could say that because he was a giver. There are some scriptures that you can not claim if you are not a giver. You do not have to give anyone one thousand dollars; just give what you can afford. Some people are just so mean. They are so unhappy with themselves they will just take your money, take your stuff, then act like they do not know you. Remember what God says, "I will bless you to because you obeyed me." If you do something in God's name you will never lose your reward.

> Hereby perceive we the love of God, because he laid down his life for us: and we ought to lay down our lives for the brethren.
> 1 JOHN 3:16

That is what Abraham did, he laid down his life. Abraham could have said Lot did this on his own. He picked Sodom even though they were wicked. He went down there and that is what he gets. There are a lot of things that we have done and God did not give us what we deserved. I have done a lot of things and God has told no one. As for me I say, *"God, thank you! I am going to pour that same love on someone else."* The best way to kill selfishness is to be generous. 1 John 3:16 says, *"…We ought to lay down our lives (soul) for the brethren."*

Jesus gave his physical life for mankind but when it comes to the lives of the brethren, it is the word soul. That means sometimes you have to be willing to lay down your plans for your brother. God does not want us to be so focused on our goals that we are not concerned about anyone else. This is very important. If we have not sown into the life of someone else, there is nothing to reap when we are down and out.

If you are 30 years old or older, you know there are some detours in life. If you are 20-something, you may not have any idea of what I am talking about because you have not lived long enough to experience life on the level of someone who is older and more mature. Okay, I understand when people say do not confess the negative, but ladies and gentlemen, we do not have to confess it because negative things will happen. It is called life! We wake up and have all these plans, go to work and then get laid off on the same day. This is why we should to invest in someone's life because God will start paying us back through the lives of other people.

It's a shame that saints can become so arrogant when the Lord blesses us. We get a raise and now we cannot speak to people. Remember when some of us did not have a suit or two pennies to rub together? Now, we are on our own two feet and cannot speak to people.

You were taking public transportation? Remember how nice you were? You were just glad to be in the house of the Lord. He met your needs day by day, but now that you have abundance, be careful!! Make yourself love others. Do you want God to give you a bonus? Bless someone who despises you!! Go directly to that person who spoke evil against you and say, "Praise God. I heard that you received a raise and I just want to bless you with this donation". God will give you a bonus.

> But whosoever hath this world's good, and seeth
> his brother have need, and shutteth up his bow-
> els of compassion from him, how dwelleth the
> love of God in him?
>
> 1JOHN 3:17

What they do not tell you on TV (and I know this by experience) is once you start prospering you have to be responsible.
And now, you are responsible for helping out your brothers and
sisters in the Body of Christ. It is no longer about YOU and
YOUR family.

Whosoever has this world's good and sees his brother has
"needs and shuts up his bowels of compassion..." I like this
scripture because John already knows that you have compassion but you choose not to share it. Do you know why?
There is no one who is full of the Spirit that does not love.
When you are full of the Holy Ghost, you are going to look
for someone to bless, even if it is just to pray for them. You
are just so full of God that you have to reach out. That is
why the Bible says that God so loved the world that He GAVE
His only begotten son. You cannot be filled with God's love
and not give. A sign that you are full of the Spirit is your
willingness to meet the needs of others. When you are full of
the Spirit, you are not worried about yourself because you
are confident that God will take care of you. Christians who
are not full of the Spirit Always worry about themselves. You
cannot be full of the Spirit and not be loving. When we walk
in love, we act like God on the Earth. God is love and we
need to show more love. Love is more than a hug. Sometimes you simply have to minister to someone. You have the
power of God on the inside of you to lead them in prayer.
You do not need a ministerial license or title to pray for people
or show concern for them.

We can be very selfish at times. When did you last help
another Person? When did you last lend money to someone
without expecting to be repaid? God is saying "until you act

as I do, I cannot trust you with the territory." Suppose God blesses you with plenty but tells you that it is not for you. How would you react?

> And when they had prayed, the place was shaken where they were assembled together; and they were all filled with the Holy Ghost, and they spake the word of God with boldness. And the multitude of them that believed were of one heart and of one soul: neither said any of them that ought of the things which he possessed was his own; but they had all things common.
> ACTS 4:31-32

> Neither was there any among them that lacked: for as many as were possessors of lands or houses sold them, and brought the prices of the things that were sold, And laid them down at the apostles' feet: and distribution was made unto every man according as he had need.
> ACTS 4:34-35

People often try to live out Acts 4:34, but they fail. They fail because they are not Spirit-driven. The key in Acts 4:31 is being filled with the Holy Ghost. When you are led by the Spirit it will kill your selfish desires. Be open to God. Selfish people walk in fear because they think that something is going to be taken away from them. That is why we purposely leave our money at home just in case they ask for a second offering at church. Do not worry about that. Where is your faith? Learn to obey so God can bless you.

> As we have therefore opportunity, let us do good unto all men, especially unto them who are of the household of faith.
> GALATIANS 6:10

The church should meet the needs of its people. As a pastor, it grieves me to see the high level of selfishness of the saints. I once asked the men of my church to help set up the runway for our fashion show and half of them walked away. People do not want to do anything without getting paid. I recently had a meeting with a lawyer to discuss our building contracts. In less than 10 minutes he'd reviewed the materials and explained what was needed. This is a man with 35 years of experience and an hourly retainer of $430, but he did not charge me for his time. Not only did he waive his fee, he also offered to be a part of the project. This is what happens when you sow into the lives of others. God may not reward you immediately, but He WILL reward you for helping others. You must reach out to people and even learn to love the unlovely.

People don't intend to be hateful, but they are distressed about the difficulties in their lives. When we are depressed, we are ME focused. All of us experience depression at times in our lives and how sad it would be if no one was available to encourage us because we failed to sow into another person's life.

> Rejoicing in hope; patient in tribulation; continuing instant in prayer; distributing to the necessity of saints; given to hospitality.
> ROMANS 12:12-13

When God motivates you to give, don't be concerned about how people will use the money. Just be obedient to God. Of course, if you know that the people involved are running a scam, just give as God directs.

Now, you may be asking yourself, "where's the balance?" The Lord says that there is nothing wrong with loving yourself, just don't be IN LOVE with yourself. We all need a healthy sense of ourselves. We should all love ourselves but not be so in love with ourselves that we are unable to release something. Let us not be so full of ourselves that we are unable to congratulate another person's achievements. Let us not be so full of ourselves that we get jealous when someone else is blessed. Some of us are so full of ourselves that we cannot humble ourselves to say "I'm sorry" when we hurt others. When we hurt others, we must go beyond asking the Lord's forgiveness to making amends with the people we've hurt. The inability to do this may very well be the reason our blessings have been held up. We cannot mistreat others and expect God to bless us.

Some of you have issues with your parents that need to be rectified. The Word says *"honor your father and mother that your days may be long in the land which the Lord thy God giveth thee"*. If you have something against your parents, settle the matter as quickly as possible. What purpose would it serve to leave the matters unresolved and then be distraught after they've passed away. We must learn that relationship is more important than being right. Your parents sacrificed in order to send you to school, but you refuse to speak to them when they disagree with you. It is their job to let you know when they believe you are going in the wrong direction. Don't allow petty disagreements to ruin your relationship with your parents/loved ones.

Your relationships are more important than material goods. What good is it to have a big mansion and there is no one to celebrate with you. What good is it to be blessed and there is no one to congratulate you? What good is it to die and no one comes to your funeral?

Put aside any differences you have with your parents, even if they weren't around as your grew up. You'll understand things better as you grow older. My father failed to support me when I was a child, but as I've grown older, I've learned to forgive him. I discussed all my issues with my father and then I chose to forgive him. I decided that I will meet his needs even though he did not meet mine. I will not allow a 20-year disagreement block my blessings.

God has you in church in order to train you to be like Joseph. God cannot bless you until you release that vengeful mentality. You limit your blessings when you refuse to speak to people. I know that some relationships have deteriorated to the point that you are simply unable to maintain a friendship, but you can still speak to people. Speak to everyone, even the phonies. Jesus instructed us to love our enemies. Don't resign from ministry because you don't get along with some of the other members. Continue with the ministry and show the devil up for what he is; a liar.

Husbands and wives should serve one another. There should never be the attitude of "I'm going to wait until he/she gives ME something". Each of you could have chosen to marry someone else. Many marriages suffer because one of the spouses is inattentive. Some couples have not been intimate for three months or more. What's wrong? Put the passion back into your marriage. Bring back the love and affection that made your house a home. Your children are there in the house starving for affection. Hug them and kiss them and let them know that you love them.

Have you ever wondered why your son lusts after other boys? It's because his father failed to show him affection. Children must receive love and affection from their parents. When fathers kiss their children, they are showing them that strength can be humble. There is nothing homosexual about a father demonstrating care or affection to his son. Let them see muscles under control. Let your son see you kiss his mother. Let your son see signs of affection throughout your house so what when he gets married, he'll know how to treat his wife.

Learn to love the saints. Why? Because you will have to live with them forever. You may as well learn to love them while on earth because you will have to live with them forever in heaven. I want my church to be more loving and I try to lead by example. Many times after I've ministered I am dead tired, but I still make it a point to speak to members of the congregation. Let us remember that we are not the only ones with difficulties. There are always others facing challenges more difficult than ours.

To open their eyes, and to turn them from darkness to light, and from the power of Satan unto
God, that they may receive forgiveness of sins,
and inheritance among them which are sanctified
by faith that is in me.

ACTS 26:18

Our inheritance is in those who are sanctified. We need to
show love now more than ever because we need each other.

Let no man seek his own; but every man another's
wealth.

1 CORINTHIANS 10:24

Even as I please all men in all things not seeking
my own profit, but the profit of many, that they
may be saved.

1 CORINTHIANS 10:33

Look not every man on his own things, but every
man also on the things of others.

PHILIPPIANS 2:4

It's not that we should not seek material gain for ourselves,
but we should also seek to be a blessing to others.

CHAPTER FOUR

Territorial Trap One:
Territory Outside of God's Will

And Abram said unto Lot, Let there be no strife, I
pray thee, between me and thee, and between my
herdmen and thy herdmen; for we be brethren. Is
not the whole land before thee? separate thyself,
I pray thee, from me: if thou wilt take the left
hand, then I will go to the right; or if thou depart
to the right hand, then I will go to the left.

GENESIS 13:8-9

The Tools for Taking Territory are:
1 Go in praying
2 Go in planning
3 Go in prepared (To work, wrestle and win.)

In this chapter, we will learn about territorial traps. I want to teach you how territorial traps hurt you and prevent you from taking your territory.

Territory is a metaphor for the things that God desires for you to possess. When we are about to take territory, God will begin to move us forward into what He desires for us to possess for such a time as this. There are obstacles, situations and circumstances that can hinder you from possessing your promised land. In these next four chapters we will talk about traps that can prevent you from taking territory.

A trap is something that you do not see. You feel like there is no harm doing something, and before long, it envelops (overtakes) you and traps you. This is how hunters catch animals. The same is true with satan. He is only doing his job by hiding the trap.

Territory Outside of God's Will

Taking territory or trying to possess something out of God's will is a major trap for Christians. As Christians, we must realize that we are not like the world. Even though we can possess in a fashion that is similar to the world, we are God's children and we walk to the beat of a different drum. We are in the world but we are not of it. Every now and then, every believer must be brought back to this spiritual fact. The number one priority for Christians is to be in God's will in everything: from our jobs, to who we choose to marry, to where we live. We are out of God's will when we make the decision to pick and choose what we want to do without first seeking and talking to God about it. God may not want us to do the things we desire to do at that time.

In Genesis 13:8, God began to bless Lot because he was connected to Abraham. Lot's herds or riches began to grow in the same way as Abraham's did. Lot was becoming so prosperous that his people started fussing with Abraham's people. Although Abraham and Lot were family, God separated Abraham from Lot. Lot was a believer, but he was carnal.

In Genesis 13:9, Abraham says, *Is not the whole land before you?* He was saying it is time to separate because he sensed God causing the separation. God will let you know when it is time to separate from people. Abraham even told Lot to choose the land he wanted to live in. Abraham did not have anything against Lot but in order to keep the peace, he knew they needed to separate.

> And Lot lifted up his eyes, and beheld all the plain of Jordan, that it was well watered every where, before the Lord destroyed Sodom and Gomorrah even as the garden of the Lord, like the land of Egypt, as you come close to Zoar. Then Lot chose him all the plain of Jordan; and Lot journeyed east: and they separated themselves one from the other.
> GENESIS 13:10-11

Sodom and Gomorrah and the surrounding cities were very beautiful and well watered. It was a tropical area, but Abraham lived in the desert. Even though people lived there, it was a desert town. In other words, Sodom and Gomorrah and those towns looked better than what Abraham had. He was going to give Lot the opportunity to pick that if that was what he wanted. Lot chose the good stuff like most of us would and this came from his desire. Most people are likely to choose what looks good to their eyes.

> Abraham dwelled in the land of Canaan, and Lot dwelled in the cities of the plain; and pitched his tent toward Sodom. But the men of Sodom were wicked and sinners before the Lord exceedingly.

GENESIS 13:12-13

What is missing in this story is that Lot never consulted the Lord. He went by his own fleshly desires. Now, ladies and gentlemen, every desire that you have does not come from the Lord. Some desires come from your flesh.

> Lot lifted up his eyes, [towards Sodom] and beheld all the plain of Jordan that was well watered every where, before the Lord destroyed Sodom and Gomorrah...
> GENESIS 13:10

In verse 12 it states, He pitched his tent towards Sodom. Lot went from looking at Sodom to moving his tent near Sodom then finally moving into Sodom. Do you know why? There was no prayer life to ask the Lord what He would have him to do. Lot was led by his flesh. Some people believe that Lot was not saved, however, Lot was saved. He believed in Jehovah God because Jesus was not on the scene yet.

> And turning the cities of Sodom and Gomorrah into ashes condemned them with an overthrow, making them an ensample unto those that after should live ungodly; And delivered just Lot, vexed with the filthy conversation of the wicked: (For that righteous man dwelling among them, in seeing and hearing, vexed his righteous soul from day to day with their unlawful deeds;)
> 2 PETER 2:6-8

Even though Lot was saved, his prayer life was very shabby. You will never read that Lot had a tight relationship with the Lord. The only time he prayed was when he asked for deliverance. There are some Christians who do not have a tight relationship with the Lord until they are about to lose their jobs, their money, their girlfriends, their boyfriends or until they have an emergency. Then they come to church and want everybody to pray for them. Lot was that kind of believer. He never asked God for His will but Abraham was blessed. Do you know why? Because everywhere he went, he built an altar. Let us look at Abraham's pattern.

> And Abram took Sarai his wife, and Lot his brother's son, and all their substance that they had gathered, and the souls that they had gotten in Haran; and they went forth to go into the land of Canaan; and into the land of Canaan they came. And Abram passed through the land unto the place of Sichem, unto the plain of Moreh. And the Canaanite was then in the land. And the Lord appeared unto Abram, and said, Unto thy seed will I give this land: and there builded he an altar unto the Lord, who appeared unto him. And he removed from thence unto a mountain on the east of Bethel, and pitched his tent, having Bethel on the west, and Hai on the east: and there he builded an altar unto the Lord, and called upon the name of the Lord.
>
> GENESIS 12:5-8

This is why Abraham was blessed. He was not blessed just because God picked him. He was blessed because he had a personal relationship with God and God ordered his steps. The issue is: are you seeking God about where you should be and where you should go? Is your territory birthed out of something you want to do? Do you think God is going to bless you? Have you prayed about the major territory you want to take? Do you really know if it is God's will? We can mess up our lives chasing the wrong thing.

In Genesis 13, Abraham makes a mistake and goes to Egypt. He had no business going to Egypt because Egypt was hit with a famine.

> And Abram went up out of Egypt, he, and his wife, and all that he had, and Lot with him, into the south. And Abram was very rich in cattle, in silver, and in gold. And he went on his journeys from the south even to Bethel, unto the place where his tent had been at the beginning, between Bethel and Hai; Unto the place of the altar, which he had made there at the first: and there Abram called on the name of the Lord.
>
> GENESIS 13:1-4

What did Abraham do? He came back, built an altar again, and called on the name of the Lord. He kept God at the center of his territory. Ladies and gentlemen, please do not make the mistake that many Christians are making. We are making all of these plans and God does not have anything to do with them. We are wondering why we are not getting blessed and why we are not prospering. It is because sometimes we are invading territory that God did not direct us to. One thing about God is that when He is giving us territory He will let us know that it is ours. When God is giving us territory, He will tell us in our spirit that it is ours before we go into any battle. I knew Southwest Philly was mine before I did anything. It's not because I am so great, but because I know what the will of God is for my life. The will of God is not easy to find and that is why we have to seek the Lord. Many Christians today do not seek the Lord.

When it comes to territory, God will let you know when the land is yours. I think this is where we copy the world too much. We are becoming more and more intellectual. Why not use intellect and follow the Spirit? Who says we cannot have both? Let's not think we are so smart that we rule out the Holy Spirit.

Remember, we can do nothing without God. If God does not blow on it, we are not going to get anything. All of our plans will not make things work. We must have the favor of God in our lives. People make plans, but things never happen for them because they lack the favor of God.

> Now Jericho was straitly shut up because of the children of Israel: none went out, and none came in. And the Lord said unto Joshua, See, I have given into thine hand Jericho, and the king thereof, and the mighty men of valour.
>
> JOSHUA 6:1-2

The lesson we learn from Joshua is that he kept his spirit open. His spirit was in tune with God and before he went into Jericho, he had the assurance that it belonged to him. He did not try to go and march around a wall without knowing that is was God's will for him. There were five kings of the Amorites who tried to come up against Israel.

> So Joshua ascended from Gilgal, he, and all the people of war with him, and all the mighty men of valour. And the Lord said unto Joshua, Fear them not: for I have delivered them into thine hand; there shall not a man of them stand before thee. Joshua therefore came unto them suddenly, and went up from Gilgal all night.
>
> JOSHUA 10:7-9

> And they went out, they and all their hosts with them, much people, even as the sand that is upon the sea shore in multitude, with horses and chariots very many. And when all these kings were met together, they came and pitched together at the waters of Merom, to fight against Israel. And the Lord said unto Joshua, Be not afraid because of

them: for to morrow about this time will I deliver
them up all slain before Israel: thou shalt though
their horses, and burn their chariots with fire.
JOSHUA 11:4-6

Joshua got the victory! You can only have faith where the
will of God is known. We cannot take territory by guessing.
We can only take territory through knowledge. We cannot
guess what we are supposed to do. That wastes time. Suppose
we do something for three years only to find out that we were
out of the will of God. Always remember that the blessing of
the Lord follows His will. It is what God wants us to do, not
what we want to do. There is much I would like to do, but I
can't because it is not God's plan for my life.

There is a reason why we claim territory. We do not claim
territory so that we can look rich and prosperous. We claim territory when it's part of God's plan. God has a purpose and we
have to stay in His will. We cannot do what we want to do. Get
on your knees and seek God, not people. Always seek God first.

Trust in the Lord with all your heart and lean not
to your own understanding.
PROVERBS 3:5A

This is what Lot failed to do. Lot did not trust the Lord,
but his own understanding. He leaned to what appeared beautiful. He was influenced by the tropical weather. He did not
consider who lived there and it was a total disaster. God in-
cinerated the whole place.

In all your ways acknowledge him and he shall
direct your paths.
PROVERBS 3:5B

How do we acknowledge God? We do this in two ways. We
do it by praying and by keeping our spirit's open. We keep our
spirits open by saying, "God, whatever you want."

Our spirits are not open if we put the brakes on. In most cases, Christians do not want to know God's will because they are scared of hearing the word "no". But let me tell you something about the word "no". When God says "no" it's because He has something better down the line. The word "no" means that God has something better than what you are able to see.

Look at the outcome of Lot's decision. The land that Lot chose, Sodom and Gomorrah, is now the Dead Sea. We cannot always make decisions based on what we see.

> Be not wise in your own eyes: fear the Lord, and depart from evil.
> PROVERBS 3:7

Always remember, acknowledgment brings assurance. When God causes us to be sure, it is that confidence that the Holy Spirit creates in our heart that will sustain us when we want to give up. This is so important. The blessed thing about assurance is that it will hold us fast. Let the winds blow; let people say what they wish. Even if the money is funny, we will know that we are in the center of God's will, and we cannot die until God fulfills His purpose in our lives. If we are doing anything major in our lives, we need to seek the Lord. God will bless us just for acknowledging Him. God loves to be chased and He loves to be sought. He wants you to chase after Him. Not just on Sunday morning, but each and every day. When did you last have a good prayer session? When was the last time you poured out your goals before the Lord?

> Wait on the Lord and be of good courage, and He shall strengthen your heart: wait, I say, on the Lord.
> PSALM 27:14

The scripture says *"He will strengthen your heart."* When we wait on the Lord, He will build that confidence in our heart. How do we know we are in God's will? When we have waited on Him and either heard His voice or felt a confirmation in our hearts. Do not listen for a voice when you are looking for the strength to go on. Sometimes God is saying, "Go ahead", but there is no confirmation for what you are about to do. There is no need to pause.

Have you ever wanted to do something, but in your spirit it just did not feel right? When we wait on the Lord, He will give us that green light. Sometimes it is not in the voice. We sometimes miss the Spirit. We cannot make God talk to us, but He has His ways of letting us know we have the green light. God often makes us pause so He can make us pray. Let me reiterate, God likes to be sought. He likes to be chased and He will sometimes say, "no" in order to keep us focused on where our blessings are coming from.

Notice what He said in Psalm 27:14, *"Wait on the Lord and be of good courage and he will strengthen your heart."* When He strengthens your heart, He gives you the go ahead and that go ahead builds courage and confidence. Everyone will think that we've made a wrong decision because they are looking at our desert land. They think we ought to pick Sodom and Gomorrah because everything there looks so beautiful, but God says "Take the desert. I want you to stay right here because I want you to watch me perform my miracle right here in the desert."

Everything that glitters is not gold. You see, in Sodom and Gomorrah there is nothing for God to do because everything has been prepared, but the desert looks bare. God is saying, "Go ahead and buy the building". I know it looks like a shack, but when I get finished with it, it will be the Taj Mahal." It is wise for us to consider how we talk about people because the one best suited for us may not always be good looking.

We seem to always gravitate towards the attractive people, but sometimes the least attractive person is the best one for us. We need to look for quality rather than quantity. That is why we need to seek God's will. It is not always the person Grandma wants for us. It will be someone connected to our purpose. *"Wait on the Lord and be of good courage and he will strengthen your heart."* He will give us the assurance that He is with us. When we get ready to take territory, we need to know that God is with us. People will come and go, but God assures us that He will not leave us and that we will make it. Since God will not leave us, we know we are blessed and have His favor. You may be all alone trying to raise your children, but I have good news for you. Be encouraged! There is a man in the house and His name is Jesus. Perhaps you can't find a good friend to talk to, but there is a friend who sticks closer than a brother. God wants us to strengthen our relationship with Him. He has always been there for us. When we sit down and negotiate a deal, God will be in the room with us.

Proverbs 14:26, says *the fear of the Lord is strong confidence*. The devil will throw everything that he can at us. When we rise up and take territory, we become a threat to hell because Satan can no longer own it. We have to tell God that we do not know what to do. He is not looking for our resumes, but our hearts. He is looking for a heart that says, "Help me." Have you ever come to that place where there was nothing else to say but "God help me?" I have been there. I did not have time to say "Jehovah Jireh, Jehovah Tsidkenu, Jehovah Rophe. God you've got to help me".

There is a difference between praying and crying out. Crying out means you really mean it.

> Cast not away therefore your confidence, which
> hath great recompence of reward.
> HEBREWS 10:35

We gain confidence by seeking God. We do not get confidence by seeking advice from someone in the "upper echelon". Now, I understand the importance of seeking wise counsel and advice, but people will often ask the Pastor, the Bishop or mentor for advice when they have already made their decision.

It is very important that we go into our territory knowing God's will for our lives. This means that we will have to take time to probe our lives with God. Do not be afraid of God. We do not have to take a territory simply because everyone else is. If God has our territory on hold, it is just not time yet. We cannot get upset because we see others possessing their land while we are kept waiting. To everything, there is a season. We have friends who've moved on and it looks like we are going nowhere, but we cannot compare ourselves to them. If we do not know God's will, we will copy them because we do not want to be left out.

Even though it looks like we are not prospering - we are. We just don't see it yet. Most people simply don't want to wait for anything, but stay in position. Get on your mark, get set, and wait until God tells you to go.

I understand that waiting brings frustration, but wait anyway. Don't rush in and make mistakes that may take years to recover. Job said *He* (God) *knows the way that I take*. Stop looking at people and look at God.

Be wise and selective about those who advise you. Many of the people who are advising you to move forward are not taking any kind of territory themselves. People do a great deal of talking, but we must be careful about whom we choose to emulate. They may not be as happy as we think they are.

Many preachers boast about all they have, but when you visit their church, you find there's not much to support the boasting.

If we are waiting for a ministry we must listen to God. Don't fret. Just wait patiently on the Lord, continue to be taught, and your turn will come.

Even those men that did bring up the evil report
upon the land, died by the plague before the Lord.
But Joshua the son of Nun, and Caleb the son of
Jephunneh, which were of the men that went to
search the land, lived still. And Moses told these
sayings unto all the children of Israel: and the
people mourned greatly.
NUMBERS 14:37-39

The people mourned because they missed their opportunity.

They rose up early in the morning got them up to the top of
the mountain and said, Look Moses, we'll be here. We'll go up
to the place that the Lord has promised. We are ready to possess the land now.

Moses says, *"Why now are you ready to transgress the com-
mandment of the Lord. But it shall not prosper."* It would not be
proper because God was not with them.

Go not up, for the Lord is not among you; that ye
be not smitten before your enemies.
NUMBER 14:42

When God is with us He won't let our enemies get the best
of us because it would make His name look bad.

For the Amalekites and Canaanites are there before you, and ye shall fall by the sword: because
ye are turned away from the Lord, therefore, the
Lord will not be with you.
NUMBERS 14:43

We can't criticize Israel because we do the same thing. God
tells us "no", but we do it anyway. The sign says "Keep off the
grass" but we walk on it anyway.

But they presumed to go up the hill top: never-
theless the ark of the covenant of the Lord, and
Moses, departed not out of the camp.
NUMBERS 14:44

The presence of God was not with them and neither was
their leader, Moses.

Then the Amalekites came down, and the
Canaanites which dwelt in that hill, and smote
them, and discomfited them, even unto Hormah.
NUMBERS 14:45

CHAPTER FIVE

Territorial Trap Two:
Tedious Talking

Now this trap really fascinated me - Tedious Talking. Tedious talking means "dangerous talking". This sounds so simple but it is so deep. This happens when people complain about where God is taking them. There is no doubt in my mind that there is a clear connection between taking a territory and the way we talk. There is a clear connection between a promise of God and how we speak.

> And the Lord said unto Joshua, See, I have given into thine hand Jericho, and the king thereof, and the mighty men of valour. And ye shall compass the city, all ye men of war, and go round about the city once. Thus shalt thou do six days. And seven priests shall bear before the ark seven trumpets of rams' horns: and the seventh day ye shall compass the city seven times, and the priests shall

blow with the trumpets. And it shall come to pass, that when they make a long blast with the ram's horn, and when ye hear the sound of the trumpet, all the people shall shout with a great shout; and the wall of the city shall fall down flat, and the people shall ascend up every man straight before him. And Joshua the son of Nun called the priests, and said unto them, Take up the ark of the covenant, and let seven priests bear seven trumpets of rams' horns before the ark of the Lord. And he said unto the people, Pass on, and compass the city, and let him that is armed pass on before the ark of the Lord. And it came to pass, when Joshua had spoken unto the people, that the seven priests bearing the seven trumpets of rams' horns passed on before the Lord, and blew with the trumpets: and the ark of the covenant of the Lord followed them. And the armed men went before the priests that blew with the trumpets, and the reward came after the ark, the priests going on, and blowing with the trumpets. And Joshua had commanded the people, saying, Ye shall not shout, nor make any noise with your voice, neither shall any word proceed out of your mouth, until the day I bid you shout; then shall ye shout.

JOSHUA 6:2-10

They had to march around the wall for six days with a closed mouth. The only thing that was to make a sound was the ram's horn. The Bible says there were two trumpets. One was the silver trumpet and the other was the ram's horn. If you blew the trumpet, it meant that a war was going on, but if you blew the rams' horn, that meant a celebration was about to take place. God says He does not want a trumpet; He wants a ram's horn.

This is an indication of our faith. The ram's horn is a symbol of celebration that we are about to take a territory. It is very important that we do not speak negatively.

> By faith the walls of Jericho fell down, after they
> were compassed about seven days.
> HEBREWS 11:30

There was a connection between their speech and their faith. In Luke 1, Gabriel appears to Zacharias and tells him that his wife is finally going to have a baby.

> And Zacharias said unto the angel, Whereby shall I know this? for I am an old man, and my wife well stricken in years. And the angel answering said unto him, I am Gabriel, that stand in the presence of God; and am sent to speak unto thee, and to shew thee these glad tidings. And, behold, thou shalt be dumb, and not able to speak, until the day that these things shall be performed, because thou believest not my words, which shall be fulfilled in their season.
> LUKE 1:18-20

Understand that there is a connection between our territory and our mouth. Proverbs 18:21 says, *Death and life are in the power of the tongue: and they that love it will eat the fruit [result] thereof.* We can talk ourselves into taking territory or we can talk ourselves out of taking territory. Once God gives us the go ahead, we must talk the way God wants us to talk because our talk keeps us focused. Even when there is no money to buy the property, the talking will keep us focused. It is how we talk. We can talk defeat or we can talk victory. We can talk depression or we can talk encouragement. It is up to us! Why not say what God says? If He said we can have it; then go tell somebody that we can have it. We can build faith in ourselves by the way we talk.

We can even motivate ourselves by the way we talk. Sometimes we cannot just think it; we've got to speak it as well. We need to let our outer ear hear what our inner ear is saying. Say to yourself, *"I am going to praise God today." "I am not going to hear a lot of junk." "This is the day the Lord has made; I will rejoice and be glad in it."* Sometimes we must encourage ourselves. As the song goes, *"Speak over yourself."* Tell yourself you are going to make it. Fill your mouth with the Word of God. Say, *"If God be for me, who can be against me. No weapon formed against me shall prosper."* Do a checkup from the neck up. What are we telling ourselves? Are we telling ourselves that we are going to make it? Are we telling ourselves "we are getting ready to go to another level?"

> Behold, we put bits in the horses' mouths, that they
> may obey us; and we turn about their whole body.
> JAMES 3:3

James said you could put a bit into a horse's mouth and the horse would obey you. As big as a ship is, it can make it through any storm based on the direction of the helm. The captain who controls the helm controls the ship. If you know how to speak, it can turn your whole life around. This is not very difficult. We do not need four years of college to do this. All we have to do is say what God says.

We need to change our speech! We can take negative words and turn them into blessings. The woman with the issue of blood kept saying, "If I could just touch the hem of His garment." "No, I am not whole yet, but I shall be." "No, I do not have it yet, but I shall see it." What pushed her to the touch? Her speech. Our speech has to push us to the touch and our touch has to push us into positive action.

Let me clarify what I am saying. Are you mostly negative or positive? When we run out of things to say, we should say "the Lord will make a way somehow". This helps us not to become legalistic. It is okay to acknowledge that we are hurting, but the full scope of our vocabulary should be toward talking to our territory. Let the positive drown out the negative.

> And Caleb stilled the people before Moses, and said, Let us go up at once, and possess it; for we are well able to overcome it. But the men that went up with him said, We be not able to go up against the people; for they are stronger than we. And they brought up an evil report of the land which they had searched unto the children of Israel, saying, The land, through which we have gone to search it, is a land that eateth up the inhabitants thereof; and all the people that we saw in it are men of a great stature.
>
> NUMBERS 13:30-32

This is where you have to watch your connections. If the people are not speaking the same language you are, cut them off. I hate to tell you this, but negative people can make us miss our destiny.

> Joshua said, If the Lord delight in us, then he will bring us into this land, and give it us; a land which floweth with milk and honey.
>
> NUMBERS 14:8

In other words, Joshua was saying, if we are in the Lord's will, He will bring us into the Promised Land. This is why we need to be connected with the right people. There may be times when we may not feel like talking positive. Let's be honest. Sometimes we are simply having a bad day. We may even be having a bad week. Sometimes we get moody. If we said we spoke positively all the time, we'd be lying. I believe in speaking positively, but I don't do it all the time. I am not a robot. I am a human being. All of us need people who can handle our bad days. We need them to encourage us and cover us on our bad days. Separate yourself from those who gossip about you and your bad days. There may be days when you begin to doubt what God has told you and you will begin to respond based on how you feel. That is the human side of you. But if you have a Caleb in your life, he can tell you that it is okay, you are going to make it. When you are connected to someone, you should be speaking the same language. You do not have to have the same personality, but God knows you must have the same spirit. If I am a bulldog, I am looking for a bulldog that will bite like I bite. I am not looking for some sleepy old dog laying in the doghouse. This is warfare!

CHAPTER SIX

Territorial Trap Three:
Tempting God

And the Lord said, I have pardoned according to
thy word: But as truly as I live, all the earth shall
be filled with the glory of the Lord. Because all
those men which have seen my glory, and my
miracles, which I did in Egypt and in the wilderness, and have tempted me now these ten times,
and have not hearkened to my voice;
NUMBERS 14:20-22

Most believers do not understand what it means to tempt
God. What is tempting God? We tempt God when we keep asking Him for miracles to see if He is qualified enough to take us
into the territory. We keep asking God for a miracle, but there
is no movement. Numbers 14 points out that it is dangerous for
believers to tempt the Lord. We all know what temptation
means; it is about the solicitation to do evil. Tempting God is a

little different. To make a long story short, the children of Israel wanted to go to the Promised Land but they were fearful and did not believe, and their unbelief angered the Lord. God was upset because He performed many miracles for them to prove that He could bring them into their Promised Land. Every miracle that comes into our lives is for God to show Himself strong and push us to the next level.

If you have just recently received Christ, this does not apply to you. Tempting God is for people who have walked with Him long enough to have experienced His glory and witnessed His miracles. When Jesus was in the wilderness being tempted by the devil, Jesus told him, *"Thou shalt not tempt the Lord thy God."* (Luke 4:12)

How many of you have seen the hand of God before? When I say 'seen the hand of God', I am going beyond Him waking you up in the morning. I am speaking of those who have walked with God, witnessed the glory cloud, witnessed the parting of the Red Sea, and seen food provided in a time of need. You've experienced the provision of God when you were unemployed and the friendship of God when you were lonely. You know that there have been bad situations and you know that had God not acted, you would have remained in that same situation. You knew it was the hand of the Lord who saved you from yourself. Do not be a silent witness to all God has done and continue to tempt Him and refuse to listen to His voice.

Why would we keep asking the Lord to do miracles when we are not going any where? That is like turning on our TV and being entertained because we have nothing else to do. God is not performing so we can applaud while He is doing miracles in our lives. He is doing miracles in our lives because He wants to take us somewhere.

What is God doing in your life? Everything that God does points to our future. If He is not doing something spectacular, He is definitely doing something supernatural. Even if God is not saying anything, everything He is doing in our lives right now is pointing to our future.

And they tempted God in their heart by asking
meat for their lusts. Yea, they spake against God;
they said, Can God furnish a table in the wilderness? Behold, he smote the rock, that the
waters gushed out, and the streams overflowed;
can you give bread also? Can he provide flesh
for his people?

PROVERBS 78:18-20

The Children of Israel wanted a miracle. They constantly mur-
mured amongst themselves, *"Can God do this?" "Can God do that?"*
How could they ask such a thing when He parted the Red Sea
and they walked right through it! We are not talking about what
He did for us decades ago. If we just focus on this year alone and
see how God has proven Himself to us, how could we ever doubt
God? When we doubt God, we tempt Him. The Israelites did
receive miracles, but they never made it to their Promised Land.
One of the reasons is that they did not want to take the risk. The
children of Israel were in their comfort zone.

We will never possess territory playing it safe. We will never
have territory sitting in a rocking chair watching T.V. We must
get up and possess the land. Many Christians want to come to
church, pay tithes, and go home. However, we will be pushed!
I thank God for the people who pushed me. We ought to thank
God for every person He sends into our lives to push us. Sports
teams have coaches who use strong words to push the players.
Coaches are not there to make things nice and easy for us. They
are there to make sure we sweat.

Taking territory is not easy. To do so you must be a pit bull,
not a poodle. We must be willing to take risks. We must be
willing to take the trip despite the turbulence. Most people are
not like that; most people do not know the Lord. We have to
make the effort to get on our knees and develop a relationship
with God. God has to be sought. *"Seek the Lord while He may be
found and call upon him while He may be near."* (Isaiah 55:6) God
likes to be chased. When we chase something it demonstrates

that we are serious. God wants to see how serious we are. God will not lead us to the next territory if we are being lazy in our current territory. We have to be willing to take a risk and put our feet in banks that are overflowing. There are some things that we must be willing to do alone without the help of our family members. God wants us to do something that no one in our family has ever done. We must develop the mentality that even if no one goes with us, we will move forward. Taking Territory is not for sissies!

CHAPTER SEVEN

Territorial Trap Four:
Tripping Into Sin

What does it mean to trip into sin? It is when our lifestyles clash with our destinies. This is a major issue with God. God is very concerned about our lifestyles because He wants us to reflect Christ in our territories. God wants to know that we will represent Him well when He gives us new land.

> And the Lord spake unto Moses, saying, Speak unto the Children of Israel, and say unto them, I am the Lord your God. After the doings of the land of Egypt, wherein ye dwelt, shall ye not do: and after the doings of the land of Canaan, whither I bring you, shall ye not do: neither shall ye walk in their ordinances. Ye shall do my judgments, and keep mine ordinances, to walk

therein: I am the Lord your God. Ye shall therefore keep my statutes, and my judgments: which
if a man do, he shall live in them: I am the Lord.
LEVITICUS 18:1-5

There are some things that are unique to us as believers that
the world knows nothing about. One is God's will. This is very
unique because the world does not care about God's will. People
say we can do whatever we want, but we as Christians cannot
do whatever we want! It is one thing to look at the world and
see their principles of success, but we cannot buy into that system. If those principles are biblical, it is okay. But when they
start deviating from the Word, we have to eat the meat and throw
away the bone. For instance, I told you about taking territory
out of God's will. We just cannot be whatever we want to be.
We must get on our knees and seek the will of God. The world
does not care about the will of God because they are not believers. But as far as we are concerned, we must practice godly
principles. This means there are certain things in a territory
that are not part of our destiny.

There are plenty of good things that are not a part of God's
plan for our lives. Many times Christians trip themselves up
because they want to do things God never told them to do. You
may have always wanted to do something to help people, and
God tells you no because that is not part of His plan for your
life. One of the greatest examples is when David wanted to build
God a house. God said, "No, you are not going to build me a
house." This is very profound because this goes to show that
we do not always get what we want. God told him, "No, you
cannot build me a house because of your purpose.

Your purpose is to have bloody hands. I called you to be a
fighter, not a builder. Your son will build. You ought to pave
the way for him because when Solomon sits on the throne, he
will not have to fight anyone.

The second unique thing about Christians is their lifestyle. It is very important that we reflect the lifestyle of Jesus Christ on our territory. Notice what God says:

> And the Lord spake unto Moses, saying, Speak unto the children of Israel, and say unto them, I am the Lord your God. After the doings of the land of Egypt, wherein ye dwelt, shall ye not do:
> LEVITICUS 18:1-3A

God is talking about the practices we had in our former lives. We cannot continue doing what we did when we were in Egypt. Whatever we came out of, we cannot go back and practice.

> And after the doings of the land of Canaan where I am going to bring you, you shall not do. Neither shall you walk in their ordinances. You shall do my judgments and keep my ordinances to walk therein. I am the Lord your God. You shall therefore keep my statutes and my judgments for if a man do, he will live in them. I am the Lord.
> LEVITICUS 18:3B-5

It is okay to better our lives, but let's seek God's agenda. Let us go back to reflecting what God wants.

> As obedient children, not fashioning yourselves according to the former lusts in your ignorance: But as he which hath called you is holy, so be ye holy in all manner of conversation; Because it is written, Be ye holy; for I am holy.
> 1PETER 1:14-16

When we get into the new land [territory], we are not to practice the things of our former land. We cannot act as we did in Egypt. Notice what God says, *"When you possess your new territory, you are not to practice the customs of Egypt; neither are you to practice the customs of your neighbors.”* (Paraphrase Leviticus 18:3-5)

God wants us to be His representatives. This is a major reason why God wants to give us territory. God's purpose in giving us new territory is not for us to make more money for us to live better. We are going to live better but that is not the motive for the believer. The believer is to reflect Christ in that new territory. God wants Christ to be exalted through the businesses that He gives us. He wants to be exalted through the beauty shops, the barbershops and the mechanic shops. The sad thing is many Christians are not even thinking about this.

As mentioned in 1 Peter 1:14-16, Peter pulls a scripture from the Old Testament in the Book of Leviticus and works it in the New Covenant. In the New Covenant, we are instructed to act like the Lord. Holiness gets a bad rap because people confuse holiness with perfection. Holiness is not perfection, but correct behavior. God is very concerned about how we will behave should He decide to give us new territory. He does not want us acting like the devil once He gives us that new business. God's purposes are very high. We are not to live holy for the sake of holiness or just because that is what we are supposed to do. We are to live holy in order to demonstrate His Kingdom on His territory. You and I have a responsibility to make sure that we show God off. What good is it for God to give us territory and we are foul mouthed? I am not trying to step on your toes. I am trying to help you so that you can take inventory. Let's examine our motives for wanting new territory. There is nothing wrong with living better; but let us understand the purposes of God. There is a motive that should be higher than just living better. That higher motive is to magnify the Lord.

> Understand therefore this day, that the Lord thy
> God is he which goeth over before thee; as a con-
> suming fire he shall destroy them, and he shall

bring them down before thy face: so shalt thou
drive them out, and destroy them quickly, as the
Lord hath said unto thee.

DEUTERONOMY 9:3

We have to understand that someone is already occupy-
ing the territory that we want to possess. God is saying He
wants to get rid of those people because they are not representing Him. It has nothing to do with how much money
they are making. The issue is they are not representing Him.
God wants them to be destroyed.

Speak not thou in thine heart, after that the Lord
thy God hath cast them out from before thee, saying, For my righteousness the Lord hath brought
me in to possess this land: but for the wickedness
of these nations the Lord doth drive them out from
before thee. Not for thy righteousness, or for the
uprightness of thine heart, dost thou go to possess their land...

DEUTERONOMY 9:4-5A

This is how I know that holiness is not perfection, but pu-
rity of heart which comes out in your lifestyle.

...but for the wickedness of these nations the Lord
thy God doth drive them out from before thee,
and that he may perform the word which the Lord
sware unto thy fathers, Abraham, Isaac, and Jacob.

DEUTERONOMY 9:5B

Let's focus on God's agenda to move Satan out of every place
and put Himself there. How does He put Himself there? He puts
Himself there through you and me. Let me tell you something,
if we are not going to straighten up our act as Christians, there
is no reason for God to give us territory. He may as well allow

Satan's kids to remain in the territory. Think about it. What good is it for God to take land from unsaved fornicators and give it to a saved fornicator? Say you are a landlord and people have destroyed your property, what good is it to have that property cleaned out only to rent it to the same type of tenant?

We are saved for a reason. We are not saved just for us to avoid going to hell. We have work to do in this world, and this work goes beyond my job. Everybody knows what the preacher is supposed to do but it is your job to know that when He saved you, you became a representative of the Kingdom of God. Everywhere you go, you are a member of the Kingdom of God. When you show up, the Kingdom should show up.

> Whatsoever city you enter and they receive you;
> eat such things that are set before you and heal
> the sick that are therein and say unto them the
> Kingdom of God is come nigh unto you.
> LUKE 10:8-9

When we heal the sick, that is a manifestation of the Kingdom of God. When we witness, that is a manifestation of the Kingdom of God. Your next door neighbors should know that the Kingdom of God is living right next door to them.

> But into whatsoever city ye enter, and they re-
> ceive you not, go your ways out into the streets
> of the same, and say, Even the very dust of your
> city, which cleaveth on us, we do wipe off against
> you: notwithstanding be ye sure of this, that the
> kingdom of God is come nigh unto you.
> LUKE 10:10-11

God needs Kingdom people in the suburbs, on City Council, in the White House and in hospitals. We need doctors who know how to pray before they operate. We need saved beauticians who will lay hands on their clients and pray for them while doing their hair. They can introduce them to Jesus and have prayer in that salon. This is why God is saying "ownership". You cannot have prayer in the salon if it is not yours; but once it becomes yours, you can represent the Lord and nobody can stop you.

If we are going to claim territory, we must claim it for the Kingdom of God. That is why God wants business owners so that we can do things the right way. We do not have to cheat, lie and connive to get the will of God done on the earth. If you own the business, then you can help someone else. That is God's agenda. Your goal is to make more money so you can relax, but God's goal is for us to make more so we can give more away. This is where our motive is all messed up. We are too materialistic in our thinking. God does not want us to make money just so we can rest on our laurels. He wants us to make more money to help others who are suffering. We should not try to claim territory if we are not concerned about helping others who may be going through trials. If our primary concern for getting rich and taking territory is not to represent Jesus or help others, we can just forget about asking God for new territory. Even wealthy unbelievers feel motivated to contribute something to others.

The two most important things about a territory are our lifestyles and our concern for people. If these two are not on your agenda then God will not be on your agenda. That is the balance between pulling God so we can get more money. Why should God give us more money if we plan to continue being selfish?

> And when he was demanded of the Pharisees, when the kingdom of God should come, he answered them and said, The kingdom of God cometh not with observation;
> LUKE 17:20

There is no Kingdom that is going to come down right now. That is in the future. You cannot see the Kingdom of God with the naked eye. Neither shall they say, *"Look over here and lo over there for behold, the Kingdom of God is within you."* (Luke 17:21) That is why God's big plan is to strategically place people so all 50 states will be covered. God wants His Kingdom representatives in every area of life. Why should God give us territory if our sole purpose is to make money without representing Him?

> Understand therefore this day, that the Lord thy God is he which goeth over before thee; as a consuming fire he shall destroy them, and he shall bring them down before thy face: so shalt thou drive them out, and destroy them quickly, as the Lord hath said unto thee.
> DEUTERONOMY 9:3

God is going to drive out the sinners because his main agenda is to establish the Kingdom of God everywhere. He wants the Kingdom of God in the projects, but He does not want us staying in the projects. He wants the Kingdom of God in the suburbs and the Cadillacs, not just in ghettos or jalopies. The higher we go in a car, the more we can prove that God is able to bring us out of the guttermost to the uttermost.

When properties become vacant, God wants us to purchase them. God just does not want to put us there so we can make more money. That is what the majority of people think. God wants to change your thinking. It goes beyond obtaining a property and getting a paycheck. If that is all we want God to do for us then He is not going to do it because He cannot trust us. God wants to move us in there so His light can shine. God says He is not going to give us a mansion if he can't trust us in the shack. You have to learn to represent Him where you are right now.

This is amazing! I hope you have enough discernment to see what is going on in America right now. There is a reason why people cannot sell their houses. How many years have the saints been hearing that the "wealth of the sinner is laid up for the just?"

We go to church and have become so religious that we dismiss half of what the preacher is saying. We are just like robots, saying "amen" when the Pastor says something. We must move beyond that.

The economy is fluctuating and we need to take advantage of the instability of the housing market. God wants us to invest in real estate, but not for us to become prideful, but to have the Kingdom of God in position to help when the saints have a need. If our hearts are not right, we are not going to do it. If we are not paying tithes now, giving God $100.00 from $1,000.00, we surely won't give $10,000 out of $100,000. God wants to give us more for less. But He does not want to give you more for less so we can show off our three fur coats. No, God says He is going to give you three fur coats so you can give one of them away. He is going to give you two cars, but one of them is not yours. He is working in you to work through you. Did you catch that? Holiness is God working in you. Territory is God working through you. We have to learn that half the stuff that comes through our hands will not be for us. We are used to everything being for us all of the time.

When you walk with God, He will let you know that you bought certain items to give them to someone else. You cannot act like it is yours because it is not. That is what taking territory is all about.

> Speak not thou in thine heart, after that the Lord thy God hath cast them out from before thee, saying, For my righteousness the Lord hath brought

me in to possess this land: but for the wickedness
of these nations the Lord doth drive them out from
before thee.

DEUTERONOMY 9:4

Do not ask God for anything if you are lying to get them.
Do not believe these people who talk about how God blessed
them. Sometimes it is not the Lord's doing, but their own
conniving, lying, cheating and scheming. If God is going to
give it to us, He is going to do it through the vehicle of righteousness. That is why it takes so long to produce because
God says He wants to give it to you the right way; not by lying
and scheming. Some people lie on their income tax by claim-
ing two children. Do not ask God for a house while you are
cohabitating with your lover. Singles are trying to claim territory by living with their lover as though they are married.
Stop trying to claim territory by giving tithes and offerings
while continuing to live a lifestyle contrary to the will of God.
God doesn't want to give you a bigger house so you can have
more parties but to establish righteousness in your life. If you
don't want to be right then you might as well work success by
fleshly standards. That is how the world does it. The world
steps on people to get what they want. They use sin to get
what they want. If we are not going to live right, what is the
difference between us and the world?

Sometimes we cannot look at the world for a pattern. Yet,
it seems that there is an ever increasing number of those in
the church who believe that success is found by doing what
unsaved people do. I want to bring the balance. There are many
unsaved people who are successful and have an abundance of
material possessions. You have Mr. Trump, P-Diddy and the
Jackson Family. How many of you know that you cannot copy
everything? You just cannot look at the world and do everything that they do. Paris Hilton and Brittany Spears are not
your examples. Russell Simmons, a practicing Buddhist, is

not an example either. How can a Buddhist who does not even believe that Jesus is the Savior be an example? How can we, being saved, look at all of these people as examples? God wants to bless us so we can be an example. Do it the right way. Do not compromise your morality to get promoted or get a raise. Do not sell out to get promoted. Saying "NO" is going to cost you. You may have to wait five to ten years versus someone who was just hired and received a promotion. Don't scratch your head at God about why they got promoted faster than you. You don't know the price they paid the night before in order to get it.

> For he that will love life, and see good days, let
> him refrain his tongue from evil, and his lips that
> they speak no guile.
> 1 PETER 3:10

Peter is quoting scripture from the Book of Psalms, *"For the eyes of the Lord are over the righteous."* (1 Peter 3:12)

Young people, stop trying to pattern yourselves after ungodly people. They do not care about God and are not promoting His righteousness. They do not care about promoting His cause so why do you want to be like them?

God needs saved role models for our young people. Our young people need to see that we can be Christians and make a good living. They need to see that we can be saved, go to school and get an education.

When are we going to stop crying that we do not have a father? I read that God is a Father to the fatherless. This encouraged my heart. He brought you into the Kingdom of God, so that He could be a Father to you.

Young people, instead of listening to all types of music on your I-Pods, download a good book and focus on your studies. Snoop-Dogg is one of the biggest porn makers around, but yet you want to pattern your life after him. We are being duped.

Satan uses celebrity lifestyles to promote his mess. God wants to promote His character and righteousness, but He needs a body to do it. God needs someone to stand up and be for real!

Here we are, exalting all of these stars just because they have money. What God wants to do is give you the money to match your lifestyle so He can get Satan off of this earth. *"Thy Kingdom come, thy will be done on earth as it is in heaven."* (Matthew 6:10)

We are in Southwest Philadelphia because His Kingdom has come and His will is being done here.

Stop imitating worldly people. There are wealthy righteous people to emulate. God is saying it's about promoting My cause. It's promoting My works and righteousness.

If God is going to give it to us, He is going to do it through the vehicle of righteousness. Righteousness always takes longer be-cause Satan is trying to tempt us between the time we pray and the time we receive the answer. The flesh does not want to wait and sometimes we will be tempted to sin in order to get what we want. When we are tempted, we have to lay down the things that tempted us and say we are not going to do them because they cause us to misrepresent God.

This means we have to act like Him. We must be full of love and compassion and walk uprightly. I am convinced that many who claim to be blessed are not blessed at all. Some have lied to get what they want. God didn't have to bless them because they manipulated things and people to get what they want.

There are saints selling out in order to become rich. There are people who cannot attend church because they have three or four jobs wanting to get rich quick. You should never sell out the will of God to get rich. God's Word tells me that *"we walk by faith and not by sight."* I am not going to take on three or four jobs and miss church just to get rich. The church is our lifeline. The church has power! The church is the reason some of us are changed today! If it was not for the church some of us would be sitting at the bar, shooting a needle in our vein, pimping or stealing. If it was not for the position God gave us in the church, we would not even be living holy. Then suddenly, when God gives us a little bit, we don't have time for the church.

Now let's talk about the saints. How can we talk about the saints when it was the saints who laid hands on us, prayed for us, and gave to us when you did not have a dime? Do you think God is going to bless you with abundance when you are cursing His body after receiving a 50 cent raise? If we cannot run with the footmen, how are we going to deal with the horses?

There is a reason why God is appearing in our bedroom and telling us to get our act together. I am speaking prophetically. He is not telling us that so we can just live right and He can take our joy. He is trying to size us up for the blessing that He has in store for us. It is more than just living right for righteousness sake. He is trying to size us up so we can take the territory. We need to be working on our habits and weaknesses. He says He pulled us out of the world so He can clean us up. He did not pull us out of the world so that we can have sloppy agape and greasy grace.

Every year you have three boyfriends/girlfriends. You are unable to maintain a relationship. God is not going to give us any territory until we can prove that He is more important than what we want.

We cannot have God's favor without His agenda. Everyone is looking for a way to be blessed even in their mess. It is impossible. We cannot keep God's favor that way. I am going to tell you something – I know how God works because I have been walking with Him for so long. Usually, the Holy Spirit puts his flashlight on some areas in our lives and that is the thing that is where we should lace our focus. If the Holy Spirit has His flashlight on the way you talk, that is the area that needs your focus. Wherever the Holy Ghost shines His flashlight is where He is telling you to get it together and that is what you should be dealing with on your knees before the Lord.

Where is the Holy Ghost flashing His light in your life? Is he trying to remove dust so that He can put some good furniture there? There is no need to ask for new territory if there will be no representation of His glory.

> Do all things without murmurings and disputings:
> that you may be blameless and harmless, the sons
> of God, without rebuke, in the midst of a crooked
> [warped] and twisted nation [generation] among
> whom ye shine as lights in the world;
> PHILIPPIANS 2:14-15

God wants us to make a difference in our generation because our generation is just what the scripture says: warped and twisted. People can practice wrong so long until they actually think its right. Did you know that if you keep using curse words you can curse without even thinking about it?

I was out of town coming out of the airport and I saw a young man wearing his pants below his derrière. I call that warped and twisted. If someone were to rob him, he wouldn't be able to run at all.

God wants to put us on display right in the middle of a crooked and perverse generation among whom we are to shine as lights in the world. Look at what it says in Deuteronomy 9:16, *"Holding forth"*. The Greek says *"holding out the word of life."*

"Holding forth the word of life." That is God's agenda. God wants to put righteousness there and that is you and me. We do not have to be perfect, but we must be blameless. What does it mean to be blameless? It means to live to the best of your ability and getting rid of the things the Holy Spirit has pinpointed in your life that are hindering your walk with the Lord.

> Ye are the light of the world. A city that is set on
> an hill cannot be hid.
> MATTHEW 5:14

God does not want us to be secret agents. He wants our neighborhood to know that we belong to Him, but half of us do not want the neighborhood to know that we belong to Him. Our neighbors ought to see us carrying our Bibles to church on Sunday.

Many of you think this isn't necessary, but this is the spiritual part of the natural that we do not want.

Practicing Muslims do not care what others think about them. They wear their garb because they are not ashamed. We should be just as unashamed about our relationship with the Lord, but it seems we are getting worse while they are getting better.

We'd prefer to hide so we do not have to be accountable for our conduct. If we're not going to be accountable to God, He might as well keep the unsaved there.

> Let your light so shine before men, that they may
> see your good works, and glorify your father
> which is in heaven.
> MATTHEW 5:16

God's agenda is that you let your light shine as you dress your children well. The world needs to see that your children are well dressed and it was not through drug money. The world should be able to come into your home and see beautiful furniture that was not purchased with money you obtained illegally.

We must have the mind of God. It is not too late to start! Let Christ shine in the apartment that you have right now. Let God clean up your act for a future blessing. Invest in your future by cleaning up right now. Do not worry about what someone else is doing. Stop justifying your behavior based on what you heard about someone else because that someone else did not die for you. That someone else did not save you and that someone else did not shed blood for you.

It should grieve our hearts to hear about marriages failing but we are fascinated by it because we too may be looking for a way out of our own marriages. Our response to the downfall of others reveals our hearts. Get on with your life and take your territory. Stop worrying about what those in leadership are not doing.

We cannot claim territory being selfish. Believers are the main ones who shoot the wounded. I think the world has more compassion for the unsaved than we do. That is why people are reluctant to discuss their problems. They know that if they do open up, their problems will be used as ammunition against them.

Why do we criticize others in church when our own lifestyles are sinful? Our own relationships are failing, so how dare we sit in judgment of someone else. Let us learn to keep our mouths closed and work on the imperfections in our own lives.

The reason some women will never have a man is because they are too busy gossiping about others. God can not give you a man when you gossip.

> But you are a chosen generation, a royal priest-hood, an holy nation, a peculiar [treasured] people; that you shall show forth the praises of him that called you out of darkness into his marvelous light.
>
> 1 PETER 2:9

Showing forth God's praises involves more than just coming to church and having a great praise and worship service. Get that out of your head. It goes beyond that. We show forth His praises by the way we conduct our lives and represent Him in our neighborhood, on our jobs, in our marriages and the way we raise our children.

When we choose not to follow God's agenda God's purposes are interrupted. Always remember this: *we live right by choice not anointing.* That means we CHOOSE whether or not to be homosexual. We CHOOSE to be married or remain single. We CHOOSE whether to stay together or divorce. We live righteous lives by CHOOSING to do so and trusting that God knows what is best for our lives.

It doesn't matter how strong the temptation, we can always CHOOSE to say NO. When we fall, we can ask God to forgive us, and clean up our territory. Do not ask God to forgive you if you plan to continue in your sinful pursuits. If you have Johnny in your bed, make Johnny get out of your bed. If you are caught up in pornography, then clean up your act and get rid of all of the smut DVDs. Do not ask God to forgive you if you have not plan to separate yourself from the things that tempt you.

I am not perfect myself, trust me. I have my own issues that I have to deal with, but the Bible teaches that we should not make provision for our flesh. Throw away the phone numbers. Tell the drug dealers that you are not going to deal with them anymore. You are a new creature. You are a representative of God and you are not going to falsify your income tax. God is tired of His children using Him like a Santa Claus.

The two most important things we must do are:
1. Live right.
2. Have concern others.

If this is not a part of our agenda, we might as well close our Bibles and live like the world. I refuse to live the way the world does. Yes, I am going to heaven but I want to be a living example on this earth.

Perhaps there is someone reading this book who wants to recommit. If there are things that you want to lay before God and your life is not where it ought to be in the Spirit of God, I want you to be bold enough to take a stand. When you do what you are supposed to do, you will be able to sleep at night and you will hear God so clearly. Some of you are not getting instructions for your purpose because things are clogging up the pipe.

Ask God to give you the strength to do what He wants you to do. When you are obedient, God will put peace in your heart.

CHAPTER EIGHT

Tools for Taking Territory:
How to Possess
Your Promised Land

To begin the process of "Taking Territory", let us first look at the scriptural foundation. Let us first look at the Book of Nehemiah:

> So the wall was finished in the twenty and fifth day of the month Elul, in fifty and two days. And it came to pass, that when all our enemies heard thereof, and all the heathen that were about us saw these things, they were much cast down in their own eyes: for they perceived that this work was wrought of our God.
> NEHEMIAH 6:15-16

The book of Nehemiah is one of the best manuals concerning building for leaders and for taking territory. If Nehemiah were here, he would tell us that we have the power to take territory. Do you believe that you have the power to take territory? If Nehemiah were here he would say, "Here are my tools." I am going to give you three tools for Taking Territory.

Tool #1: When you take the territory, go in praying.

When Nehemiah received a burden from the Lord to take territory, he automatically went into prayer. Before we take the territory, before we get more money, before we buy bigger houses, let us say, "Hey, the first thing I am going to do is pray." Let this year be the year that you decide that you are going to pray more.

> And they said unto me, The remnant that are left of the captivity there in the province are in great affliction and reproach: the wall of Jerusalem also is broken down, and the gates thereof are burned with fire. And it came to pass, when I heard these words, that I sat down and wept, and mourned certain days, and fasted, and prayed before the God of heaven,
> NEHEMIAH 1:3-4

Before we take territory, we need to stop and pray. Why should we pray?

We need to pray over territory to get God's perfect will. It may be that we are attempting to claim a territory that does not belong to us. How did Nehemiah know that he was called to take that territory? The answer is in verse 4. When he heard the word, he sat down, wept and mourned. Do you know why he sat and mourned? He had a burden. That burden became his knowing and it was the burden that led him to pray. Burdens lead to burning. His soul was burning; this moved him to do what he had to do.

> These are thy servants and thy people, whom thou hast redeemed by thy great power, and by thy strong hand. O Lord, I beseech thee, let now thine ear be attentive to the prayer of thy servant, and to the prayer of thy servants, who desire to fear thy name: and prosper, I pray thee, thy servant this day, and grant him mercy in the sight of this man. For I was the king's cupbearer.
> NEHEMIAH 1:10-11

The whole chapter was on prayer. We must understand that if we take territory, whether it is a business, ministry, or whatever God has led us to do, prayer is a fundamental thing. Knowing God's will is the thing that is going to see us through when the storms hit. If we endeavor to take territory and do not pray, we will not be able to stand when the storm hits.

Whenever we step out and take territory, Satan is going to show up. We are going to need both the spiritual and the natural because when we pray, we open the door for the miraculous. Prayer is the miracle for taking territory.

Point #1 – Pray to get God's <u>Perfect Will</u>

Let us not forget, Nehemiah is a cupbearer. Nehemiah does not have any money! We who have a plan but no money are in good company! Nehemiah did not have money or workers. His job was to taste the wine for the King before he drank it. This means if Nehemiah drank the wine and it was poisonous, he would be the one to die. Nehemiah was a cupbearer and a slave. When it is God's will for us to take territory, He will use us no matter what.

Point #2 – Pray to get God's <u>Provision</u>

> And it came to pass in the month of Nisan, in the twenthieth year of Artaxerxes the King, that wine was before him: and I took up the wine, and gave it unto the king. Now I had not been beforetime sad in his presence.
>
> NEHEMIAH 2:1

In Chapter Two, there are four months of silence. Four months of doing nothing but serving the King. That shows us that delay is not denial. When we pray about territory, it does not mean that we are going to jump into it tomorrow.

> And it came to pass in the month of Nisan, in the twentieth year of Artaxerxes the King, that wine was before him: and I took up the wine, and gave it unto the king. Now I had not been beforetime sad in his presence. Wherefore, the king said to me, why is thy countenance sad, seeing thou art not sick? This is nothing else but sorrow of heart. Then I was very sore afraid,
>
> NEHEMIAH 2:1

"Then I was very sore afraid." Do you know why he was scared? It was going to cost him his life because he was not supposed to frown in the presence of the King. Even when we have a bad day we have to put on a happy face.

> And said unto the king, Let the king live for ever:
> why should not my countenance be sad, when the
> city, the place of my fathers' sepulchers, lieth waste,
> and the gates thereof are consumed with fire? Then
> the king said unto me, For what dost thou make
> request? So I prayed to the God of heaven.
>
> NEHEMIAH 2:3-4

What was he praying for? He was praying for favor. First,
Nehemiah was praying for God's will. He knew what God's will
was. He just didn't know how to go from being a cupbearer to a
contractor. He needed God's favor.

> So I prayed to the God of Heaven. And I said unto
> the king, If it please the king, and if thy servant
> have found favour in thy sight, that thou wouldest
> send me unto Judah, unto the city of my fathers'
> sepulchers, that I may build it. And the king said
> unto me, (the queen also sitting by him,) For how
> long shall thy journey be? and when wilt thou
> return? So it pleased the king to send me; and I
> set him a time.
>
> NEHEMIAH 2:4B-7

The favor of God was working! I like Nehemiah because
he is very smart. Nehemiah waited four months for his opportunity to speak. He said, *"Let me get in all that I need."*
First, I am going to pray for His perfect will. Second, I am
going to pray for God's provision.

Point #3 – Pray to get God's <u>Protection</u>

Nehemiah had to pray for God's protection because he realized that when he stepped out, folks were not going to like it. They would try to kill him and wipe him out.

> But it came to pass, that when Sanballat heard that we builded the wall, he was wroth [angry], and took great indignation, and mocked the Jews. And he spake before his brethren and the army of Samaria, and said, What do these feeble Jews? Will they fortify themselves? Will they sacrifice? Will they make an end in a day? Will they revive the stones out of the heaps of the rubbish which are burned? Now Tobiah the Ammonite was by him, and he said, Even that which they build, if a fox go up, he shall even break down their stone wall.
> NEHEMIAH 4:1-3

Notice what Nehemiah said, *"Hear, O our God."* He prayed. He prayed for protection.

> Hear, O our God; for we are despised: and turn their reproach upon their own head, and give them for a prey in the land of captivity.
> NEHEMIAH 4:4

> But it came to pass, that when Sanballat, and Tobiah, and the Arabians, and the Ammonites, and the Ashdodites, heard that the walls of Jerusalem were made up, and that the breaches began to be stopped, then they were very wroth, And conspired all of them together to come and to fight

against Jerusalem, and to hinder it. Nevertheless we made our prayer unto our God, and set a watch against them day and night, because of them.
NEHEMIAH 4:7-9

And I looked, and rose up, and said unto the nobles, and to the rulers, and to the rest of the people, Be not ye afraid of them: remember the Lord, which is great and terrible, and fight for your brethren, your sons, and your daughters, your wives, and your houses. And it came to pass, when our enemies heard that it was known unto us, and God had brought their counsel to nought, that we returned all of us to the wall, every one unto his work.
NEHEMIAH 4:14-15

That is what prayer will do – confuse the enemy. Prayer will give you the strength to keep on working and it will confuse the enemy. It will produce a secret while we are building and our enemies will wonder how we can take a "lickin' and keep on tickin'." Our prayer life is vital. If we are going to take territory, Nehemiah's example teaches us that we have to pray.

Tool # 2 – Go to Planning

Prayer is the *miracle* for taking territory but planning is the *mechanics*. This is where the rubber meets the road. People pray all day but don't devise any plans. I believe the reason some of us fail to see what we need despite having prayed is that we haven't done enough moving. When we take territory we cannot just spend the day praying. We must get strength from that prayer and start planning.

Taking territory is not for the lazy. We have to get dirty plus work hard

> The preparations of the heart in man, and the answer of the tongue, is from the Lord.
>
> PROVERBS 16:1

What are the preparations of the heart? The answer is the planning.

> Commit thy works unto the Lord, and thy thoughts shall be established.
>
> PROVERBS 16:3

What are "the thoughts"? They are our plans. Without our plans, there is nothing to commit to the Lord. Do you know what Nehemiah was doing in the four months of silence? He was planning! Do you want to know what he was doing before he obtained favor? He was planning! So, before our miracle comes, do the mechanics! This is where everybody goes silent. We have to organize. Organizing will prepare us for opportunities.

What did Nehemiah do in his planning? He did two things. He looked at his situation and laid it out. I do not know about you, but I love this! He looked at what he had to deal with. If you are going to take a territory, you have to look at what you have to deal with. If you are going to get out of debt next year, review your credit report. If you are going to believe God for a healing, look at what the doctor's report says. Don't pretend it doesn't exist because it does.

> So I came to Jerusalem, and was there three days. And I arose in the night, I and some few men with me; neither told I any man what my God had put in my heart to do at Jerusalem: neither was there any beast with me, save the beast that I rode upon. And I went out by night by the gate of the valley, even before the dragon well, and to

the dung port, and viewed the walls of Jerusalem, which were broken down, and the gates
thereof were consumed with fire.
NEHEMIAH 2:11-13

We do not know how to take territory because we do not
want to look at the negative. Before a positive can be built, sometimes we have to look at the negative. We have to look at what
has been destroyed in our lives. We have to look at a negative
situation and speak "positive" over it.

And I went out by night by the gate of the valley,
even before the dragon well, and to the dung port,
and viewed the walls of Jerusalem, which were
broken down, and the gates thereof were consumed with fire. Then I went on to the gate of the
fountain, and to the king's pool: but there was no
place for the beast that was under me to pass.
NEHEMIAH 2:13-14

When we have a vision, we cannot focus on how bad things
seem because we can see the end from the beginning. Nehemiah
looked at the negative but planned the positive. That is what
we must do today. Look at the negative and plan the positive.

Then went I up in the night by the brook, and
viewed the wall, and turned back, and entered
by the gate of the valley, and so returned. And
the rulers knew not whither I went, or what I
did; neither had I as yet told it to the Jews, nor
to the priests, nor to the nobles, nor to the rulers, nor to the rest that did the work.
NEHEMIAH 2:15-16

Look at the wisdom in that scripture. When we get to see the work, we cannot take a lot of people with us. When you go to look at something negative, do not take a lot of people with you because they will tell you that you cannot do it. Take someone with you who has already accomplished something. Take someone who can reassure that you can do it. Nehemiah didn't tell the nobles, rulers or anybody because he did not want to be talked out of it.

> Then said I unto them, Ye see the distress that we are in, how Jerusalem lieth waste, and the gates thereof are burned with fire: come, and let us build up the wall of Jerusalem, that we be no more a reproach.
> NEHEMIAH 2:17

Yes, go and look at it! Don't continue looking at it negatively because you know there is something better to come out of it. I know there is something better. There is something better than what we have been through in the past. This is the Year of Better Things. It is a new beginning. In other words, the pages of your life are about to turn and God is about to write something new.

Go ahead and look at the credit report. But whose report will you believe? Believe the report of the Lord! Go ahead and look at the doctor's report; *"but he was wounded for my transgressions, bruised for my iniquities, the chastisement of my peace was upon him and by his stripes I am healed!"* (Isaiah 53:5) What I like about Nehemiah is his prayer life. It caused him to believe that he could do it. It is our prayer life that will cause us to believe that we can do it. This is something our families never did.

Saints of God, stop running from the negative. How many of you have pictures in your houses? Do you know where the pictures came from? The pictures came from a negative. You have got that nice picture hanging on the wall. Do you know how that picture was produced? It was produced from a negative in the dark. When did Nehemiah do his search? He went out at nighttime. It was not in the daytime when he looked at that negative situation. It was at night. Nothing can come out of a picture unless it is developed in the dark. Last year may have been your night, but bless God, this year you are stepping out of darkness into His marvelous light. Step out! Step out! You can do it! You can do all things through Christ. Through Christ, not your checkbook, your job, or what you know, but through Christ! All you need is a dream!

Look at your negative and your positive. Look at the negative and tell it that it will never enter your life ever again! Last year, you cried and asked "God, Why?" This year is "How Lord?" How do You want this thing to come to pass? How do You want me to do it? How should I plan it? Pull those bills out and tell those bills that you will be in the black. Speak to the red. You are going to be black.

First, Nehemiah looked at it. Then he laid it out. You cannot lay it out if you do not look at it.

What do you mean he laid it out? I mean he organized it. He organized his way out. He did not just pray and look at soap operas. I believe his prayer was, "God just give me wisdom. How will I get this wall up?" Give me wisdom on how to take my territory. Give me wisdom to deal with my territory. Give me wisdom! Look at it and lay it out.

In Chapter 2, Nehemiah looked at it and Chapter 3 he laid it out. There are two major words in Chapter 3 that tells me how he laid it out. The two words are: *"built"* and *"repaired."* He built and repaired.

> Then Eliashib the high priest rose up with his brethren the priests, and they builded the sheep gate; they sanctified it, and set up the doors of it; even unto the tower of Meah they sanctified it, unto the tower of Hananeel. And next unto him builded the men of Jericho. And next to them

builded Zaccur the son of Imri. But the fish gate
did the sons of Hassenaah build, who also laid
the beams thereof, and set up the doors thereof,
the locks thereof, and the bars thereof. And next
unto them repaired Meremoth...
NEHEMIAH 3:1-4A

Throughout the third chapter we find the word *built* or *repaired*. That is what we have to do. Look at the ruins and get some wisdom to repair it. Whatever we cannot repair, we build. Building is something we have never done before. Repairing is that which is messed up that God is going to reshape.

Sometimes, there are things in our lives that need to be reshaped. For example, look at some of your relationships. Sometimes God won't allow us to leave, but will have us repair them. You may not have even been speaking to each other earlier in the year, but now things are going well. I am talking to you married folks now. The reason God has not brought some things to pass in your marriage is because you are not flowing together as a unit. I said this is the year of flow because, if you flow, God will let it go. Go from ruin to repair. Go from rubbish to building.

Tool #3 – Go in Prepared

Nehemiah would tell you to go in prepared if you are going to take your territory. Nehemiah took his territory because he was prepared to take it. Being prepared is the mental toughness we will need because taking territory is not easy. Yes, we are going to dance and shout, but when that dancing and shouting is over, we are going to have to do something. When the children of Israel crossed the Red Sea, they broke out in a shout, but when it was time to wait on God, they were not mentally tough. We have to be mentally tough to take a territory. We have to be mentally tough in three areas:

A. Be Prepared To Work.

If we want our territory, we have to take it. Notice what I said, "Taking Territory." It will not be given to us and there are those who don't want us to have it. So we have to be mentally tough to take it. Be prepared to work. Be prepared for sleepless nights because you are praying and planning. Be prepared to take half the money and put it on the territory. Be prepared to put some of your other dreams on hold for your major dreams. Be prepared for all the lazy people to leave you because once you start working you won't have time to talk on the phone as you once did. They will stop calling you. Be prepared for the criticism. Be prepared for the people who will accuse you of being arrogant. "Who do you think they are?" "I am a man/woman taking my territory.

> Then I told them of the hand of my God which was good upon me; as also the king's words that he had spoken unto me. And they said, Let us rise up and build. So they strengthened their hands for this good work.
> NEHEMIAH 2:18

> So built we the wall; and all the wall was joined together unto the half thereof: for the people had a mind to work.
> NEHEMIAH 4:6

> Yes, also I continued in the work of this wall, neither bought we any land: and all my servants were gathered thither unto the work.
> NEHEMIAH 5:16

Nehemiah wanted everyone to know that he did not just sit at home and watch T.V. Let me give you a warning. God is not going to give us extra help until He sees we are doing something. This is for those who are crazy enough to believe God and start out by themselves. As my grandmother said often, "If you take one step; God will make two."

Be prepared to wrestle because it is not easy. Do you know why you have got to be the one? It is because it is your territory. Don't be angry because people won't see your territory the way you see it. That is your baby. It is in your heart. It will not be in everyone else's heart. Sometimes, God assigns people to help you get started and then they walk away. It is called scaffolding. They help you to scaffold the work. They do not stay to help you forever. You are the one who is pregnant and must carry the baby. Remember to thank everyone who helped you, even if all they did was give you $5.00. If they leave you, say thank you for the time we had together. Good God Almighty! Be prepared to work.

B. Be Prepared To Wrestle.

I repeat, taking territory is not easy. Sometimes it will be easier to shout all night than to get up the next morning. Be prepared for doors to be slammed in your face. Be prepared for the word "No". We are going to hear "no" every now and then. We are going to hear "Sorry" every now and then. Like I said, "Be prepared to wrestle and not take no for an answer." Pin that *no* down with a *yes*. We are going to replace everybody that left us. They are going to leave us because they are not long-term people. It does not mean they are bad; they are just not in it for the long-term. Be prepared to wrestle.

You cannot say I am looking for a miracle and then roll over and go to sleep. You must work hard. Taking territory is not for the lazy. Be prepared to cry sometimes and be prepared for the negative.

As negative forces come, we must always believe that God is with us. He is the one who holds the paintbrush in His hand and writes His plan for our lives on the canvases of our hearts. Without this, we have no direction, no purpose and no roadmap. Having His plan serves as our blueprint for possessing our land and fulfilling the promises that He gave each of us. I wish there was a special prayer we could use to erase all the negativity that exists in our lives. Unfortunately, we must fight through it all, knowing that "this territory is mine!"

About the Author

Dr. Jimmie A. Ellis, III, the dynamic Senior Pastor of Victory Christian Center, is both recognized and respected for his standard of excellence in ministry. He is a highly sought after speaker who is anointed in the areas of teaching, leadership, mentoring and fatherhood.

Dr. Ellis possesses an extraordinary revelation of the Word of God. His dynamic yet practical teaching style has led many to give their lives to Jesus Christ. His life-changing teachings on holy living, home and marriage, purpose and financial freedom are empowering generations.

Raised in the Mount Olive Apostolic Church, under the pastorship of Dr. John Myers, Dr. Ellis accepted Jesus Christ at the age of nine. By age twelve, Dr. Ellis began teaching Bible study. In 1983, he was released to pastor.

He then founded the Bible Enlightenment Philadelphia Christian Center with just 7 members. Today that humble beginning is known as Victory Christian Center, a thriving ministry located in the heart of Southwest Philadelphia with a membership of over 2,000.

Today, under the covering of Bishop Don Meares of Evangel Temple in Upper Marlboro, MD, Dr. Ellis serves on the Advisory Board of the International Congress of Local Churches (ICLC).

Having a heart for leaders, Dr. Ellis formulated the Victory Fellowship of Local Churches to provide pastors with mentoring, building church leadership and forming a network of covenant relationships with like-minded men and women of God. His annual leadership conferences and workshops are highly demanded. He has also ordained and fathered several men and women into their own ministries.

In 1985, Dr. Ellis founded Arnaz Ministries School of the Word Bible Institute. As Founder and President, Dr. Ellis designed a curriculum to train individuals who've been called to a five-fold ministry, the ministry of counseling, and those who desire an in-depth study of the Word of God for spiritual fulfillment. Today, the two-year program offers a variety of selective and innovative courses conducive to developing church leaders of all facets.

In 1999, Dr. Ellis founded The Conquerors Community Development Corporation (CCDC), a mission designed to elevate the quality of life for the Southwest Philadelphia community through economic development, child development, technological awareness, spiritual/cultural programs and health initiatives. Dr. Ellis' vision is to further institute employment services, daycare services, housing and community revitalization programs, health related projects and life skills to empower the community.

In March 2004, Dr. Ellis received his honorary Doctorate of Divinity Degree from Saint Thomas Christian College in Jacksonville, Florida. Dr. Ellis' contributions have been applauded throughout the city by the media, governing officials and with numerous awards.

To order additional copies of

Taking Territory

have your credit card ready and call
1 800-917-BOOK (2665)

or e-mail
orders@selahbooks.com

or order online at
www.selahbooks.com

Printed in the United States
136424LV00003B/2/P